Henry H. (Henry Hopper) Miles

Canada East at the International Exhibition

Henry H. (Henry Hopper) Miles

Canada East at the International Exhibition

ISBN/EAN: 9783742839336

Manufactured in Europe, USA, Canada, Australia, Japa

Cover: Foto ©Andreas Hilbeck / pixelio.de

Manufactured and distributed by brebook publishing software
(www.brebook.com)

Henry H. (Henry Hopper) Miles

Canada East at the International Exhibition

CANADA EAST

AT THE

INTERNATIONAL EXHIBITION.

CATALOGUE OF PRODUCTS FROM CANADA EAST,

"MEDALS" AND "HONORABLE MENTIONS" AWARDED TO CANADA,

AND THE

DECLARATION OF PRIZES TO THE COLONIAL EXHIBITORS, JULY 11, 1862.

TO WHICH IS ADDED

A SUCCINCT ACCOUNT OF **THE EASTERN TOWNSHIPS** OF LOWER CANADA.

BY

HENRY H. MILES, M.A.
COMMISSIONER FOR CANADA AT THE INTERNATIONAL EXHIBITION,
LONDON, 1862.

INTERNATIONAL EXHIBITION, 1862.

COMMISSIONERS FOR CANADA IN LONDON.

SIR W. E. LOGAN,* *Chairman.*   B. CHAMBERLIN, ESQ., *Secretary.*

PROF. H. H. MILES.   J. B. HURLBURT,† ESQ.

Mem. The Exhibition was also visited by the following gentlemen, appointed by the Canadian Government.

COLONEL THOMPSON, of the Canada Board of Commissioners—also a Juror—
     (returned to Canada after the Distribution of Awards on July 11th.)

W. BOWMAN, ESQ., Honorary Commissioner.

COLONEL RHODES,   „   „

T. KEEFER, ESQ.,   „   „

MAJOR CAMPBELL,   „   „

* Also a *Juror*—returned to Canada on leave, after the Distribution of Awards, July 11th.
† Also a *Juror*—duties as Commissioner ceased from the Distribution of Awards, July 11th.

A CATALOGUE

OF THE

PRODUCTS OF CANADA EAST,

AT THE

INTERNATIONAL EXHIBITION, LONDON, 1862.

N.B.—The names of Exhibitors to whom *Medals* and *Honourable Mentions* were awarded by the International Juries have the letters **M** and **H M** respectively prefixed.

OBJECT.	EXHIBITED BY	LOCALITY AND REMARKS.
1. Economic Minerals, Rocks, Metallic Ores, Metals, &c. &c.		
Bog iron ore . . . 3 pieces ready for furnace Washed bog ore . . . Slag from the smelting . 5 qualities of pig iron, one piece re-cast . . 1 railway wheel . . . 3 nail rods . . . Horse-shoe nails . . . Piece scythe iron . . „ „ *hammered* . 1 pair railway wheels that have run 150,000 miles .	M—A. La Rue and Co., Three Rivers . .	Procured from the neighbourhood of the St. Maurice and Batiscan Rivers for the Radnor forges ; about 2000 tons annually produced.
Specimens, magnetic iron ore.	Geological Survey of Canada . . .	*Hull*, Lot 11, range 7 ; and *Grenville*, Lot 3, range 3.
Specimens, bog iron ore	„ „	*Vaudreuil*,—contains 50 per cent of iron.
„ „	„ „	St. Vallier, county Bellechasse.
Specimens, red hematite .	„ „	*Sutton*, Eastern Townships, Lot 9, range 11, and Lot 6, range 9.—20 to 50 per cent of iron.
Specimens of hematite .	„ „	*Brome*, Eastern Townships, Lot 3, range 1.—40 per cent.
Magnetic iron ore .	„ „	*Sutton*, Eastern Townships, Lot 9, range 9.—38 per cent.
Galena, undressed lead ore } Hand-picked prills . }	C. C. Gloster, Gaspé .	*Indian Cove*, Gaspé.
Undressed lead ore . .	James Wright and Co. .	*Upton*, Eastern Townships.
Specimen of ilmenite .	Geological Survey of Canada . . .	St. Urbain,—composed of *oxide titanium*, of *iron*, and *magnesia*.
Yellow sulphuret of copper	G. B. Moore and Co. .	*Upton*, Eastern Townships, Lot 51, range 20.—14 per cent.
„ „	Geological Survey of Canada . . .	Bissonette's mine, *Upton*, Eastern Townships, Lot 49, range 20.—10 per cent.

OBJECT.	EXHIBITED BY	LOCALITY AND REMARKS.
Minerals, &c.—*continued.*		
Variegated sulphuret copper	H M— W. H. A. Davies,	Acton Mine, *Acton*, Eastern
„ „ jigged .	and C. Dunkin . .	Townships, Lot 32, range 3,
„ „ rough		about 17 per cent of copper.
dressed		
„ „ tye work		
Waste from the tyes		
Polished slab of the ore		
Rock of the country		
Plan of the mine.		
Sulphurets of copper . .	Pomroy, Adams, and Co.,	Wickham Mine, *Wickham*,
Plan of the mine, by Messrs.	Sherbrooke, Eastern	Eastern Townships, Lot 15,
Willson and Robb . .	Townships . . .	range 10—30 per cent.
Yellow sulphuret of copper	Pomroy, Adams, and Co.,	Yale's Mine, *Durham*, Eastern
Plan of the mine by Willson	Sherbrooke, Eastern	Townships, Lot 21, range 7,
and Robb . . .	Townships . . .	supposed to belong to the
		same band as the Acton
		Mine
Yellow sulphuret of copper	Shaw, Bignol and Hunt,	Black River Mine,*St. Flavien.*
	Quebec . . .	
Variegated and vitreous sul-	M—English and Cana-	Harvey's Hill mine, *Leeds*,
phuret of copper . .	dian Mining Co., Que-	Eastern Townships, Lot 13,
	bec	range 15.
„ „		
„ from lowest bed		
„ from highest bed		
„ dressed		
Plan of the mine.		
Yellow sulphuret of copper	Flowers, Mackie and Co.	St. Francis Mine, *Cleveland*,
Plan of mine, by Willson		Eastern Townships, Lot 25,
and Robb.		range 12.
Variegated and vitreous sul-	Griffiths and Brothers,	Jackson's Mine, *Cleveland*,
phurets of copper . .	Sherbrooke, E. T. .	Eastern Townships, Lot 26,
		range 13.
Variegated sulphurets of cop-	Flowers, Mackie and Co.	Coldspring Mine, *Melbourne*,
per		Eastern Townships, Lot 6,
Plan of mine by Willson and		range 2.
Robb.		
Variegated and vitreous sul-	H M—Sweet and Co.,	Sweet's Mine, *Sutton*, Eastern
phurets of copper, from a	North Sutton, E T.	Townships, Lot 8, range 10.
bed.		
Plan of mine, by Mr. Rich-		
ardson.		
Vitreous sulphuret, with	G. D. Robertson and Co.	Craig's Mine, *Chester*, Eas-
green carbonate of copper		tern Townships, Lot. 8,
		range 5.
Sulphurets of copper. . .	Geological Survey of Ca-	Nicolet Branch Mine, *Ham*,
	nada.	Eastern Townships, Lot 28,
		range 4, abundant water
		power near, for crushing
		and dressing the ore.
Copper pyrites with iron. .	„ „	*Garthby*, Eastern Townships,
		Lot, 22, range 1.
Yellow sulphuret of copper	H M—Tho. McCaw, Len-	Haskell Hill Mine, *Ascot*,
from a bed.	noxville, E. T.	Eastern Townships, Lot 8,

OBJECT.	EXHIBITED BY	LOCALITY AND REMARKS.
Minerals, &c.—*continued.*		
Plan of mine, by Willson and Robb.		range 8, Ore from this mine without any dressing, has been sent to Boston, and yielded on an average about 8 per cent. pure copper
Sulphuret of nickel .	Geological Survey of Canada.	*Orford,* Eastern Townships, Lot. 6, range 12.
Native gold . . .	" "	Fief St. Charles, C. E.—
Stream gold in nuggets .		*Nine,* among the nuggets,
Stream gold in dust . .		weigh from 10 dwts. to 126 dwts.
Stream gold—a nugget with quartz	" "	Vaudreuil, C. E.—the nugget weight 80 dwts.
Auriferous blende .	" "	Rapids of the Chaudiere, C. E.—Occurs in a vein with galena, &c., the vein from 2 to 3 feet thick.
Grains of gold in bitter-spar	" "	*Leeds,* Eastern Townships, Lot 15, range 14.
Grains of Platinum and of Iridosmine	" "	Fief St. Charles, C. E.—Separated from gold dust found in the drift.
Chromic iron .	" "	Mt. Albert, *Gaspè.*
Chromic iron .	" "	*Ham,* Eastern Townships, Lot 4, range 2—the bed 14 inches thick.
Specimen of chromic iron .	" "	*Bolton,* Eastern Townships, Lot 23, range 6.
Specimen of chromic iron .	Benj. Walton, Montreal	*Melbourne,* Eastern Townships, Lot 23, range 6.
Molybdenite . .	" "	*Quetachoo river,* Manicouagan Bay, C.E.
Dolomite . .	" "	*Brome,* Eastern Townships, Lot 16, range 11.
Magnesite . .	" "	*Sutton,* Eastern Townships, Lot 12, range 7.
Magnesite . .	" "	*Bolton,* Eastern Townships, Lot 17, range 9.
Soapstone (steatite) . .	" "	*Bolton,* Eastern Townships, Lot 24, range 4.
Cut specimens of soapstone	" "	*Sutton,* Eastern Townships, Lot 12, range 7.
Potstone (compact chlorite)	" "	*Bolton,* Eastern Townships, Lot 26, range 2.
Uncut specimens *mica rock*	" "	*Shipton,* Eastern Townships, Lot 18, range 5.
Cut and dressed plates, *mica* and crystals of do. . .	" "	Grenville.
Specimen of *plumbago* .	Russell and Co. .	Pointe du Chêne Graphite Mine, Argenteuil, C.E.
Specimen of plumbago .	Geological Survey of Canada	Grenville, C.E.
Specimen of plumbago .	A. Cowan . . .	Lochaber, C.E.
Asbestus from a vein . .	Geological Survey of Canada	St. Joseph, C.E.

OBJECT.	EXHIBITED BY	LOCALITY AND REMARKS.
Minerals, &c.—continued.		
Specimen of clay and pottery made from do.	Michael Finley, Quebec	St. Foy, near Quebec.
Cube foot of dressed lime-stone	C. E. Cheeseman, Phillipsburg . . .	Phillipsburg, St. Armand.
Do. „	Geological Survey of Canada . . .	Caughnawaga, C.E.
Do. „	„ „	St. Dominique.
Do. „	„ „	Pointe Claire.
Do. „	„ „	Montreal.
Do. „	„ „	Chevotriere
A foot cube of dressed sand-stone	„ „	Augmen. of Grenville.
Do. „	„ „	Quin's Point.
A foot cube of dressed Labra-dorite	„ „	Abercrombie.
A foot cube of dressed gneiss	H. O'Donnell, Quebec .	Jeune Lorette.
Do. „	Geological Survey of Canada	Grenville.
A foot cube of dressed syenite	„ „	Grenville.
Do. „	„ „	Grenville.
A foot cube of dressed granite	„ „	St. Joseph.
Do. „	„ „	*Barnston*, Eastern Townships.
Yellowish white marble .	„ „	Grenville, C.E.
Spotted green and white marble	„ „	Aug. of Grenville, C.E.
White marble . . .	C. R. Cheeseman, Phillipsburg	Phillipsburg, St. Armand.
White marble . . .		
White and green marble .		
Dove-grey marble . .		
Black marble . . .	Geological Survey of Canada	St. Armand.
Red and veined marble .	„ „	St. Joseph.
Grey marble . . .	„ „	Caughnawaga.
Grey and red spotted marble	„ „	
Dove-grey marble . .	„ „	St. Dominique.
Drab marble . . .	„ „	Esquimaux Island.
Brownish black marble .	„ „	Pointe Claire.
Greenish black marble .	„ „	
Grey marble . . .	„ „	Montreal.
Do. . . .	„ „	
Specimen of cream-white marble, striped with yellow	„ „	*Dudswell*, Eastern Townships, Lot 23, range 7. Excellent and beautiful marbles obtainable here. The dark grey sometimes resembles the Portor marble from Italy. The streaked and spotted are thought by some to excel the celebrated *Egyptian*.
Dark grey and yellowish marble		
Fawn, yellow, and white marble		
Brecciated and green serpentine marble	„ „	*Orford*, Eastern Townships, Lot 6, range 13.
Light green marble .		
Dark green, and striped marble	„ „	*Orford*, Eastern Townships, Lot 12, range 8.

OBJECT.	EXHIBITED BY	LOCALITY AND REMARKS.
Minerals, &c.—*continued.*		
Green and white serpentine marble	Benj. Walton, Montreal	*Melbourne,* Eastern Townships, Lot 20, range 5.
Dark and light green serpentine marble		
Brecciated green serpentine marble	Geological Survey of Canada	*Melbourne,* Eastern Townships, Lot 20, range 5.
Brecciated green serpentine marble with white veins	„ „	St. Joseph.
Specimens of roofing slate .	M—B. Walton, Montreal	*Melbourne,* Eastern Townships, Lot 32, range 6. Excellent slate, equal to the best Welsh and French. Supplied in upwards of 20 different sizes for roofing, and placed on the railroad cars at prices from 2 to 4 dollars per square of 100 feet. Far less costly for roofing than tin or iron, and only about one-third more than common wooden *shingles.*
Specimens of roofing slate .	Geological Survey of Canada	*Orford,* Eastern Townships, Lot 2, range 5.
Do. „	„ „	*Tring,* Eastern Townships.
Do. „	„ „	*Kingsey,* Eastern Townships, Lot 4, range 1.
Do. „	„ „	*Cleveland,* Eastern Townships, Lot 6, range 15.
Raw cement stone .	„ „	Hull, C. E.
Do. „	„ „	Magdalen River.
Raw limestone . . .	„ „	Montreal.—About 270,000 bushels per annum manufactured—price about 8d. sterling per bushel.
Prepared lime . . .		
Red bricks	„ „	St. Jean.—About 2,000,000 have been made there in a year.
Common red bricks .	Peel & Compte, Montreal	Montreal.—6,000,000 annually, at 5$ to 6$ per 1000.
Common building bricks .	H M—Bulmer and Sheppard, Montreal.	Montreal.—6,000,000 annually, at prices from 5$ to 12$, according to form of brick.—Boaden's machine used.
Pressed front do.		
Radiating front do.		
Circular do.		
Clay used in making sewerage pipe tiles	H. O'Donnell, Quebec .	Quebec.—Used for main sewers and house drains. More than 150,000 laid in Quebec.—Price, according to diameter, 8d to 4s 6d sterling per linear foot.
A six-inch sample of pipe tile		
Cut whetstones . . .	Geological Survey of Canada.	*Stanstead,* East Townships, Lot 15, range 1.
Do. „	„	*Hatley,* Massawhippi Lake, Eastern Townships.

OBJECT.	EXHIBITED BY	LOCALITY AND REMARKS.
Minerals, &c.—*continued*.		
Cut whetstones . . .	Geological Survey of Canada	*Bolton*, Eastern Townships, Lot 23, range 6.
Do. „	„ „	*Kingsey*, Eastern Townships, Lot 7, range 2.
A Buhrstone, dressed . .	„ „	Grenville, C. E., Lot 3, range 5.
Specimen of marl . .	„ . „	Montreal.
Do. „	„ „	Anticosti.
Do. „	„ „	St. Armand.
Brownish iron ochre . .	E. Caron . .	St. Anne de Montmorenci.
Brownish black do.		
Yellow ochre		
Green and yellow ochres .	Geological Survey of Canada.	Cap de La Madelaine.
Purple and yellow ochres .	„ „	Pointe du Lac.
Cut and polished specimens of Labradorite . . .	„ „	Abercrombie, C. E.
Cut and polished specimens of Epidosite . . .	„ „	Shickshock mountain, Gaspé.
Sandstone, for glass making .	„ „	Williamstown, Beauharnois.
Specimen of peat . .	„ „	Chambly, C. E.
2. Agricultural Products.		
Half bushel, Canadian barley	Agricult. Society, county Beauharnois.	Grown by John Galbraith.
„ two-rowed English barley . .	„ „	„ Dugald Thompson
Half bushel, English oats .	„ „	„ David Benning.
„ early peas	„ „	„ Jos. Geudron.
„ late do. . .	„ „	„ John Brodie.
„ autumn rye .	„ „	„ J. B. Feliatreau.
„ black sea wheat	„ „	„ Charles Tait.
„ wheat .	„ „	„ — Mc Donald
„ flax seed . .	„ „	„ M—Celestin Bergeoin.
„ Timothy grass seed	„ „	„ M—Charles Tait.
Half bushel, two-rowed barley	Agricultural Society of Huntingdon . .	„HM—M. McNaughten, 45 bushels per acre.
„ Indian corn	„ „	Grown by S. Schlinger, 25 bushels per acre.
„ oats . .	„ „	Grown by J. Muir, 80 bushels per acre.
„ peas . . .	„ „	M—Grown by John Porcil, 40 bushels per acre.
„ wheat .	„ „	Grown by P. McFarlane, 25 bushels per acre.
„ barley .	M—*W. Boa*, St. Laurent, Montreal . . .	30 minots per arpent.
„ beans . .	„ „	
„ Indian corn	„ „	50 minots per arpent.
„ white corn .	„ „	
„ potatoe oats .	„ „	
„ early Canada peas	„ „	
„ Black Sea wheat	„ „	25 minots per arpent.
„ buck wheat .	„ „	

OBJECT.	EXHIBITED BY	REMARKS.
Agricultural Products—*continued.*		
Samples, Indian corn meal .	W. *Boa*, St. Laurent, Montreal	
„ oat straw .		
Half-bushel, barley .	P. *Beaudry*, St. Damase	30 minots per arpent
„ Black Sea wheat	F. *Beaudry*, St. Damase	15 „ „
One bushel, barley .	H M—*James Logan*, Petite Côte . .	
„ Horse beans .	„ „	
„ Two rowed maize	„ „	
„ Oats .	„ „	
„ Spring wheat .	„ „	
1 crock of butter .	„ „	
Half-bushel, barley .	P. *Malo*, St. Damase .	30 minots per arpent.
„ Black Sea wheat	G. *Malo*, St. Damase	15 „ „
„ Barley .	D. *McKinnon*, Somerset, Eastern Townships .	35 bushels per acre
„ Fife wheat .	„ „	32 „ „
„ Variety ditto .	„ „	
Sample, bearded wheat .	„ „	30 bushels per acre
Half-bushel, barley .	*Antoine Rocheleau*, St. Bruneau	
Samples of flax .	„ „	
„ of wool .		
Half-bushel, barley .	H M—*C. Wilkins*, Rougemont . .	27 min. per arpent
„ Indian corn .	„ „	36 do. „
One box, maple sugar . .		
Half bushel, Canada beans .	M—*W. Evans*, Montreal	
„ Broad Windsor do. .	„ „	
„ Dwarf Marrowfat peas	„ „	
„ White Canada do. .	„ „	
„ Black-eyed do. . .	„ „	
„ Early field do. . .	„ „	
„ Coffee do. . .	„ „	
Half bushel Timothy grass seed	„ „	
6 ears Indian corn (white) .	„ „	
„ „ (red) .	„ „	
30 lbs. Maple sugar . .	M—*D. Brown*, Cowansville, Eastern Townships	Unrefined, as usually made by farmers
1 Cheese . .	„ „	
Sample, 2 varieties *clover* .	*Lymans, Clare, and Co.* Montreal . .	
„ Flax seed . .	„ „	
„ Timothy grass seed		
One trace, *Indian corn*	*Pierre Martin*, St. Laurent	
One bale, *hops* (1861)	*Thos. Dawes and Son*, Lachine	
Half bushel, oats	H M—*T. Badham*, Drummondville, Eastern Townships	
Half bushel, oats	H. Mathieu, St. Hyacinthe	30 min. per arpent.

OBJECT.	EXHIBITED BY	REMARKS.
Agricultural Products—*continued.*		
Half bushel, peas	*Henry Cumming.* Megantic, Eastern Townships	
Specimen maple sugar	H M—Rev. F. L'Heureux, Verchéres	
One box, maple sugar	*J. B. Alix,* St. Césaire	
Half bushel, buckwheat	L. Brunelle, St. Hyacinthe	50 min. per arpent.
Half bushel, spring wheat	*Jas. Drummond,* Petite Côte	
Half bushel, wheat	*John Drummond,* Petite Côte	
Half bushel, wheat	*J. Lamonde,* St. Damase	15 min. per arpent.
Half bushel, wheat	*D. Stewart,* Inverness, Eastern Townships	25 bush. per acre.
III. Products of Forests and Waters.		
1. Woods.		
Specimens of 73 varieties, with branches, leaves, and flowers	M—*The Abbé Provancher,* St. Joachim	The numerals printed on *white* paper
„ of 74 woods	H M—*F. F. Prieur,* St. Vincent de Paul	„ on *green* paper
„ of 71 „	*J. B. Le Page,* Rimouski	„ on *yellow* paper
„ of 73 „	*Dr. Dubord,* Three Rivers	„ on *pale rose* colour
„ of 72 „	*David Price,* Chicoutimi	„ on *red* paper
„ of 72 „	H M—C. E. Coutlée	„ on *blue* paper
Specimens of 23 kinds of squared timber, with 20 do. of pine and spruce planks and staves	M—Messrs. Duncan, Patton and Co., Quebec	Collected in the Quebec market
Specimens of sawn woods	H M—Geo. Giugras, Quebec	
2. Pharmaceutical Products.		
Canada balsam . . .	Mr. Olivier Giroux, Druggist, Quebec . .	Gum of Balsam Fir extracted from Black Spruce, for making Spruce and Beer
Spruce oil . .	„ „	
Extract of spruce . .	„ „	
Canadian Sarsaparilla . .	„ „	
Gold thread (Coptis Trifolia)	„ „	
Wild endive (Cichorium intybus)	„ „	
Canadian Dragon's Blood (Sanguinaria Canadensis) .	„ „	
Wild anice root (Anychia Canadensis) . . .	„ „	
Ginseng (Panax quinquefolium) . . .	„ „	
Winter green (Pyrola umbellata) . . .	„ „	
Capillaire (Adiantum pedatum) . . .	„ „	
Castoreum (in its natural state) . . .	„ „	
Cod liver oil . . .	„ „	

OBJECT.	EXHIBITED BY	REMARKS.
Products, &c.—*continued.*		
3. Preserved Fish.		
Smoked Salmon . . .	Messrs. Turgeon and Ouellet, Merchants, Quebec . . .	
Salted Salmon . . .	,, ,,	
Smoked Herring . . .	,, ,,	
Salted Labrador Herring .	,, ,,	
Salted Herring (from Bay Chaleurs) . . .	,, ,,	
Salted Rimouski Herring .	,, ,,	
Salted Cod . . .	,, ,,	
Salted Eel . . .	,, ,,	
Salted Sardine . . .	,, ,,	
4. Substances obtained from Cetacea and Fish.		
White porpoise skins .	Mr. C. H. Tetu, River Owelle, county of Kamouraska.	Two sides, undressed.
Skins of seal. . .		Two, in their natural state.
Oil of white porpoise .		
Oil of shark . .	,, ,,	
Cod liver oil . .	,, ,,	
5. Furs.		
Skin of moose deer .	Mr. Olivier Côte, of Quebec	Undressed.
Skin of bear . .	,, ,,	
Skin of red fox . .	,, ,,	
Skin of black martin .	,, ,,	
Skin of beaver . .	,, ,,	
Skin of pecan . .	,, ,.	
Skin of racoon . .	,, ,,	
Skin of mink . .	,, ,,	
Skin of otter . .	,, ,,	
Skin of Canadian lynx .	,, ,,	
Skin of skunk . .	,, ,,	
Six skins of musk rats .	,, ,,	
Skin of marmot . .	,, ,,	
6. Birds.		
One case containing 103 specimens of birds found in Canada East . .	HM—Jas. Thomson, Esq. Montreal . . .	
Specimen of weasel (Mustela vulgaris) . . .	,, ,,	
Red squirrel (Sciurus Hudsonius) . . .	,, ,,	
IV. Manufactured Articles.		
1. Chemical Products		
1 dozen arctusine . .	S. J. Lyman and Co., Montreal	
2 lbs. Canadian yellow wax .	,, ,,	
Toilet soap . . .	J. Wheeler, jun. Montreal	In glass case.
2. Substances used for Food.		
2 smoked hams . .	M—G. Reinhart, Montreal	Prices attached, from 5½d to
2 dried bacon hams .	,, ,,	7½d for the ham and bacon;
1 piece smoked beef .	,, ,,	10d per lb. for the beef.

OBJECT.	EXHIBITED BY	REMARKS.
Manufactured Articles—*continued.*		
1 piece smoked bacon	G. Reinhart, Montreal	Prices attached, from 5¼d to
1 piece dried bacon	„ „	7½d for the ham and bacon;
2 bologna sausages	„ „	10d per lb. for the beef.
2 cases wine	N. Pigeon, Montreal	From Canadian wild grape; price attached 4s 2d per gallon.
Forest wine	Madame Paulet, Montreal	From Canadian wild grape; price 4s 2d per gallon—1s 8d per bottle.
3. Railway Plant.		
Railway wheels from Radnor forges, St. Maurice	M— A. La Rue and Co., Three Rivers	Have run 150,000 miles in a post office car of the G. T. Railway.
Improved railway wheel, from the Radnor forges	„ „	Pattern now in use on G. T. R. and G. W. R. of Canada.
Model of direct action, self-balanced oscillating cylinder	Joshua Lowe, G. T. R. of Canada East	For locomotive, marine, or stationary engine.
4. Carriages.		
A four-wheeled open carriage	Clovis Leduc, Montreal	Price attached, £90.
5. Manufacturing Machines and Tools.		
Brick and Tile making Machine, small Model of Pug Mill	W. Bawden, Hochelaga, Montreal	
Model of Improved Water Wheel	H M — E. O. Richard, Quebec	
6. Agricultural and Horticultural Machines and Implements.		
An Iron Plough	M— J. Jeffery, Coté de Nieges, Montreal, C. E.	
An Iron Swing Plough	M—J. Paterson, Montreal	Price attached, 10 guineas.
7. Philosophical Instruments and Processes.		
Diagram of mean diurnal changes of temperature, of air and water of the river St. Lawrence	T. D. King, Montreal	
8. Photography.		
A case containing two portfolios of Photographs	M—W. Notman, Montreal	The Bird's-eye maple case was made by J. and W. Hilton of Montreal, and silver-mounted by R. Heudery, Montreal. The portfolios are the work of J. Lovell, Montreal. The Portfolios are labelled *Canada East* and *Canada West* respectively.

OBJECT.	EXHIBITED BY	REMARKS.
Manufactured Articles—*continued.*		
9. Surgical Instruments.		
Apparatus for detecting consumption and testing the lungs . . .	G. S. D. Bonald, Medical Student, McGill University, Montreal .	With an illustrative diagram.
10. Woollens, &c.		
2 lbs. woollen yarn .	M—Mrs. P. Dunphy, St. Malachi . . .	
5 pieces Canadian tweed .	M—Wm. Stephen and Co., Montreal . .	
1 piece Canadian spring tweed	„ „	
1 piece of check . .	„ „	Prices attached, from 2s 6d
1 piece Etoffe (light) .	„ „	to 3s 6d per yard.
11. Paper, Stationery, Printing and Bookbinding.		
1 ream printing paper .	Angus and Logan, Montreal . . .	
1 ream Manilla paper .	„ „	
12. Educational Works and Appliances.		
Collection of 17 School and Text books, printed in Canada . . .	M — Hon. P. O. Chauveau . . .	Approved, according to law now in operation, by the council of Public Instruction, as class books in schools in Lower Canada.
Journal de l'Instruction Publique and Journal of Education for the years 1857, 1858, 1859, 1860 and 1861, 5 sets . . .	„ „	The sets are in paper and in cloth boards respectively.
Rapport sur l'Instruction Publique, and Report on Education in Lower Canada for the years 1855, 1856, 1857, 1858, 1859, and 1860	„ „	
Acts of the Provincial Parliament concerning Education and Schools in Lower Canada, 2 copies in each language . . .	„ „	
3 sizes of desk and seat for schools . . .	„ „	Made by W. Allen, Montreal, approved by the Council of Public Instruction and in use in the schools.
12. Furniture, &c.		
Samples of 18 kinds of brooms, whisks, and dusters	M—W. Nelson & Wood, Montreal . . .	Classified as *extra* and *common*—prices attached to the latter from 1s 6d to 9s 3d per dozen.

OBJECT.	EXHIBITED BY	REMARKS.
Manufactured Articles—*continued.*		
13. Iron and General Hardware.		
3 sheets of nail-plate from "Canadian Pig Metal," "Scotch Pig Metal," and "Scrap Iron" . . .	H M—W. H. Snell, Victoria Iron Works, Montreal, C.E. . . .	Puddled
3 pieces of iron, cut ready for nail machine . . .	" "	
A chain of cut nails . .	" "	Bent when cold, showing their extreme *toughness.*
14. Pottery.		
Specimen of drain-tiles .	M—Missisquoi Tile and Drain Co., C.E.	
15. Manufactures not included in previous classes.		
1 fount of Long Primer, Roman	C. T. Palsgrave, typefounder, Montreal.	Price per lb. attached, 1s 6d
2 type cases	" "	
Stand for cases . .	" "	
Specimen impression in frame	" "	
Cigars of Canadian manufacture, 9 kinds . .	P. Henry, Montreal, C.E.	Prices attached; from £5. 3s 8d to £16. 11s 8d per 1000.
16. Architectural Drawings.		
View of the Lower Canada Industrial Exhibition Building at Montreal . .	J. W. Hopkins, architect, Montreal, C.E. . .	The Exhibition held during the visit of H.R.H. the Prince of Wales. Frame of inlaid Canadian woods, by J. Guidi, Montreal.
Interior view of a skating rink	Lawford & Nelson, architects, Montreal, C.E.	Erected for the Victoria Skating Club, Montreal.
Photographs of the Liverpool and London Assurance Office, Montreal, and of the new Unitarian church .	Hopkins, Lawford and Nelson, architects, Montreal, C.E. . . .	Photographed by Notman, Montreal.
17. Oil Paintings.		
View of the Shawenagan Falls, on the St. Maurice River, Canada East . . .	O. R. Jacobi, Montreal, C.E.	The property of A. J. Pell, by whom the frame was carved and gilt. Price, with frame, 200 guineas.
View on the St. Maurice River, Canada East . .	" "	The property of A. J. Pell. Price 50 guineas.

NOTE.—The prices are stated in sterling money ; and those attached to articles of commerce whose value is fluctuating, were the market prices in Canada in March 1862.

A LIST OF
THE AWARDS TO CANADA.

NOTE.—This List is not confined to successful Exhibitors from Canada East, but includes those belonging to *both* sections of the Province.

	NAME OF EXHIBITOR AND AWARD.	OBJECT REWARDED, AND REASONS.
CLASS I. Mining, Quarrying, Metallurgy, and Mineral Products.	**Medal.** Billings, E., of the Geological Survey	For his published decades on Canadian fossils, and his valuable general contributions to palæontology.
	English and Canadian Mining Company Eastern Townships, C.E.	For the skill and perseverance with which they have opened their ground, and the discovery of deposits conformable with the stratification.
	Foley and Co.	For plans of mines, ores, and lead, smelted in the colony.
	Hunt, T. Sterry, of Geological Survey	For the instructively-described series of the crystalline rocks of Canada, and his various published contributions to geological chemistry.
	La Rue and Co., Three Rivers, Canada East.	For excellent cast iron railway wheels from bog iron ore which have run 150,000 miles.
	Montreal Mining Company.	For interesting series of copper ores, accompanied by plans and sections of the workings.
	Taylor, A.	For good specimens of crude and prepared gypsum, with plans and section of the gypsum mines.
	The Officers of the Geological Survey of Canada.	For an admirably prepared collection of specimens, illustrating the mineral resources of the province.
	Walton, R., Melbourne Eastern Townships, C.E.	For the discovery of good roofing slates.
	West Canada Mining Company.	For specimens and plans illustrating a well worked copper mine.
	Williams, for Canadian Oil Company.	For introducing an important industry by sinking artesian wells in the Devonian Strata for petroleum.
	Honorable Mention. Davies, W. H. A., Acton, Eastern Townships, C.E.	For interesting and instructive specimens from a remarkable deposit.

	NAME OF EXHIBITOR AND AWARD.	OBJECT REWARDED, AND REASONS.
CLASS I.—*continued.* Mining, Quarrying, Metallurgy, and Mineral Products.	Hon. Men.—*continued.* McCaw, T., Ascot, Eastern Townships, C.E.	For fine and instructive specimens of ores, running with the stratification and illustrating the structure of the country.
	Sweet, S. and Co., Sutton, Eastern Townships, C.E.	For fine and instructive specimens of ores, running with the stratification, and illustrating the structure of the country.
CLASS II. SECTION A. Chemical Products.	**Medal.** Benson and Aspden .	Samples of Indian corn starch. For the excellent quality of samples.
	Canadian Oil Works .	For an extensive exhibition of the derivatives of petroleum.
	McNaughton, E. A.	Flour and potato starch—for the excellent quality of samples.
	Pearson, Brothers . .	For an extensive exhibition of the derivatives of petroleum.
CLASS III. Substances used for Food. SECTION A. Agricultural Produce.	**Medal.** Agricultural Board of Upper Canada . .	For samples of wheat from various counties, of excellent quality.
	Agricultural Society of Huntingdon, one medal to grower, Canada East	For peas, 40 bushels per acre, grown by John Percil.
	Agricultural Society of Wellington . .	For wheat of excellent quality.
	Agricultural Society of Wentworth and Hamilton, (three medals for growers) . .	For blue-stem wheat grown by J. H. Anderson; for red chaff wheat grown by John Smith; for potatoe oats grown, by A. Gorie. Very superior in quality.
	Boa, W., Canada East .	For all his samples in collection.
	Denison, R. L. . .	Indian corn stalks. For extraordinary growth.
	Evans, W., Canada East	For collection of grains and seeds, excellent and interesting.
	Fleming, J. . .	For seeds and grains, as excellent and interesting.
	Johnstone, B. .	For sample of Soule's winter wheat, of excellent quality.
	Logan, J., Canada East .	For spring wheat of excellent quality.
	Peel (County) Agricultural Society—Medal to John Lynch, Secretary . . .	For barley, peas, and two kinds of spring wheat, all of excellent quality.
	Shaw, A. . . .	For rye of excellent quality.
	Agricultural Society of Beauharnois, Canada East (two medals to growers) . .	For flax seed grown by C. Bergoin; for grass seed grown by C. Tait.
	Wilson, J. . . .	For oatmeal of excellent quality.

	NAME OF EXHIBITOR AND AWARD.	OBJECT REWARDED, AND REASONS.
CLASS III. Substances used for Food.	**Honourable Mention.** The Agricultural Society of Huntingdon, Canada East	For barley grown by Mr. McNaughton.
	The Agricultural Society of Wentworth and Hamilton	The collection of wheats. Goodness of quality.
	Badham, F., Eastern Townships, Canada East	For oats of good quality.
	Logan, J., Canada East	For barley. Goodness of quality.
	Shaw, A.	For Indian corn and marrowfat peas, excellent quality.
	Wilkins, C., Canada East	Indian corn, goodness of quality.
SECTION B. Grocery and Preparations of Food.	**Medal.** Brown, D., Cowansville, Eastern Townships, Canada East	Maple sugar. Excellence of quality.
	Reinhart, G., Montreal, Canada East	Hams. Excellence of quality.
	Honourable Mention. L'Heureux, Rev. F. L., Canada East	Maple sugar. Illustrative.
CLASS IV. Animal and Vegetable Substances used in Manufactures.	**Medal.** Blaikie and Alexander	For dressed flax.
	Bridge, Andrew	For a tub on a new principle of construction, exhibiting much taste and ingenuity.
SECTION C. Vegetable Substances used in Manufactures.	Eddy, E. B., Ottawa	For machine-made wooden pails and tubs—at exceedingly low prices.
	Ingersoll, C. Lewis	For a cask constructed on a new and ingenious principle, for live liquids.
	Laurie, James	For planks and logs, and 21 named specimens of woods from Ontario district.
	McKee, Hugh	For a scientifically-named collection of 98 of the woods of the colony, accompanied with leaves, &c.
	Moore, T.	For a large collection of excellent handles for tools and implements in hickory and other woods.
	Nelson and Wood, of Montreal, Canada East	For whisks and brooms of Sorghum straw, at very low prices, from 1s 6d to 6s per dozen.
	Patton, Duncan and Co., Quebec, Canada East	For 19 very fine squared logs of timber.
	Provancher, the Abbé, Canada East	For a very extensive, accurately named, and extremely well illustrated collection of the woods of

D

NAME OF EXHIBITOR AND AWARD.	OBJECT REWARDED, AND REASONS.
CLASS IV.—*continued.* Animal and Vegetable Substances used in Manufactures.	
Med.—*continued.*	the colony, accompanied with dried specimens, useful information, &c.
Sharp, Samuel . .	For a magnificent collection of planks, polished slabs, veneers, and a named collection of 26 specimens, all from the Western districts.
Skead, James .	For a magnificent collection of planks, logs, and a scientifically named collection of 37 woods, all from the Ottawa district.
Van Allen, D. R. . .	For planks and logs, all magnificent specimens, from the Thames district, and 21 scientifically named specimens.
Trembiscki, A. L. . .	For magnificent logs of white oak, rock elm and hickory.
Honourable Mention. Bronson, A. . .	For magnificent sections of Strobus and white oak.
Burrows . .	For fine sections of "Landrus sassafras."
Choate, Jacob . .	For fine cherry-wood and soft maple plants.
Coutleé, Canada East .	For named collection of 72 woods of the colony.
Gingras, G. Quebec, Canada East . .	For fine planks of timber.
Crooks, Miss . .	For collection of 490 native plants.
Prieur, F. X., Canada East . .	For a named collection of 74 woods of the colony.
Rose, E. H. . .	For a box of very fine black walnut veneers.
CLASS V. Railway Plant.	
Medal. La Rue and Co., Three Rivers, Canada East .	Cast Iron Hollow Wheels. For excellence of material.
Honourable Mention. Sharp, S. . . .	Model of sleeping and freight cars.
CLASS VIII. Machinery in General.	
Honourable Mention. Richard, E. O., Quebec, Canada East .	Model of water-wheel.
CLASS IX. Agricultural and Horticultural Machines and Implements.	
Medal. Gaskin, Capt. P. .	For his collection of Agricultural tools.
Joffry, J., Canada East .	For his iron plough.
McSherry, J. . .	For his iron plough.
Morley, J. . .	For his iron plough.

	NAME OF EXHIBITOR AND AWARD.	OBJECT REWARDED, AND REASONS.
Class IX.—*continued.* Agricultural and Horticultural Machines and Implements.	**Med.**—*continued.* Paterson, J., Montreal, Canada East	For his iron plough.
	Whiting and Co. . .	For their collection of agricultural tools.
	Honourable Mention. Sovereign, L. L. . .	For his combined cultivator and drill.
	Collard, H. . .	For his cultivator.
CLASS X. Civil Engineering, Architectural and Building Contrivances. SECTION A.	**Medal.** Brown, J. . . .	For the excellence of manufacture of his hydraulic cement.
	Stephenson, G. R., as representative of his cousin the late R. Stephenson, M.P., F.R.S.	For the extraordinary boldness of conception and the great ingenuity of the construction of the Victoria Bridge, Montreal, Canada East.
	Honourable Mention. Bulmer and Sheppard, Montreal, Canada East	For the excellence of their bricks.
	Gibb, T. . . .	For the excellence of his white bricks and drain tiles.
	Missisquoi Drain Tile Company, Canada East	Drain tiles of good quality.
	Betts, E. L. . . Hodges, J. . . Peto, Sir S. M., Bart., M.P. . .	A collective honourable mention for the successful execution of the Victoria Bridge, and for the ingenuity displayed by Mr. Hodges in constructing the coffer-dams for the same.
CLASS XIV. Photography.	**Medal.** Notman, Montreal, Canada East . .	For excellence in an extensive series of photographs.
CLASS XXI. Woollen and Worsted, including mixed Fabrics generally.	**Medal.** Mrs. Dunphy, St. Malachie, Canada East, and W. Stephen and Co., Montreal, Canada East	For the display of woollen goods and hand-spun yarns manufactured in the colony.
CLASS XXIX. Educational Works and Appliances.	**Medal.** Chauveau, Hon. P. O. Canada East . .	For the merit of his educational journals and reports.
	Passmore, S. W. . .	For his collection of birds and fish.
	Honourable Mention. Thomson, James, Canada East . . .	For his collection of birds.

AWARDS TO CANADA.

	NAME OF EXHIBITOR AND AWARD.	OBJECT REWARDED, AND REASONS.
CLASS XXXI. Hardware. SECTION A. Manufactures in Iron.	Honourable Mention. Snell, Victoria Works, Canada East . .	For good machine-made nails.
CLASS XXXII. SECTION B. Cutlery and Edge Tools.	Medal. Gaskin, Capt. R. . . Tongue and Co. . .	Collection of agricultural hand-implements. Assortment of edge tools, highly finished.

Note.—In connection with the foregoing lists of Products exhibited from Canada East, and of the Awards gained by Exhibitors from both the Upper and Lower Sections of the Province, it may be interesting to some of our Canadian friends to be informed of a few additional particulars, relating to the principles by which the decisions of the International Juries were governed,—and also to know the results with respect to the numerous other Colonies which have taken part in the great competition.

There is therefore appended a brief account of some of the formal proceedings on the day of the Distribution of Awards, which it is hoped may be found to include all that is necessary in view of the purposes named.

THE DECLARATION OF PRIZES

AWARDED BY THE INTERNATIONAL JURIES

TO

COLONIAL EXHIBITORS.

A Grand State Ceremonial for the Declaration of Prizes to Exhibitors was appointed to be held on Friday, July 11th. On the morning of that day an official programme of proceedings was issued, indicating that H.R.H. The Duke of Cambridge, as Her Majesty's Representative, would make known the Jury Awards at certain Stations within the Exhibition Building. Station No. III., at the Victoria Gold Trophy, was assigned to the Colonial Commissioners, and here the following representatives of Colonies and Miscellaneous Foreign Stations were directed to assemble before 1 o'clock, P.M.

COLONIAL COMMISSIONS.

INDIAN EMPIRE.

*Dr. Forbes Watson.**   A. M. Dowleans, Esq.

1.—NORTH AMERICAN COLONIES.

CANADA.

Sir W. E. Logan, F.R.S.   Professor Henry Miles.
Brown Chamberlin, Esq. B.C.L.
J. B. Hurlburt, Esq. LL.D.

VANCOUVER ISLAND.

Alfred John Langley, Esq.   John Lindley, M.D. F.R.S., Superintendent
                        of Colonial Departments at the Exhibition.
                        Richard Charles Mayne, Esq.

BRITISH COLUMBIA.

Capt. Mayne, R.N.   John Lindley, M.D. F.R.S.

NEW BRUNSWICK.

Thos. Daniel, Esq.   R. Rankin, Esq.
Hon. John Robertson, Esq.   Richard Wright, Esq.
James Brown, Esq.

* The names of the Chairmen for the day are printed in *itali.*

NOVA SCOTIA.

Andrew M. Uniacke, Esq.
Rev. G. Honeyman.
Thomas Q. Grassie, Esq.

Arthur M. Wier, Esq.
Henry Baggs, Esq.

PRINCE EDWARD'S ISLAND.—H. Haszard, Esq.

NEWFOUNDLAND.—F. N. Gisborne, Esq.

BERMUDA.—W. C. Fahie Tucker, Esq.

2.—WEST INDIAN COLONIES, &c.

BAHAMAS.—Samuel Harris, Esq.

BARBADOES.—Stephen Cave, Esq. M.P.

BRITISH GUIANA.

Sir Wm. H. Holmes.

A. F. Ridgway, Esq.
Joseph T. Gilbert, Esq.

DOMINICA.—P. L. Simmonds, Esq.

JAMAICA.

His Excellency C. H. Darling.
Sir Joshua Rowe, K.C.B.
Thomson Hankey, Esq. M.P.
Wm. Smith, Esq.

Wm. Cunningham Glen, Esq.
Edward Chitty, Esq.
Lucas Barret, Esq. F.L.S. F.G.S.
Alex. F. Ridgway, Esq.

ST. VINCENT.—George C. Stacpoole, M.D.

TRINIDAD.

Wm. Rennie, Esq.

Sir W. H. Holmes.

3.—AFRICAN COLONIES AND COUNTRIES.

NATAL.—W. C. Sargeaunt, Esq.

ST. HELENA.—N. Solomon, Esq.

LIBERIA.

Gerard Ralston, Esq.
Samuel Gurney, Esq. M.P.
Thos. Hodgkin, M.D.
Edwin Fox, Esq.

Rev. Alfred Crummell.
Thos. Clegg, Esq.
Mr. Ex-President Roberts.
Mr. Marshall.

4.—AUSTRALIAN COLONIES.

NEW SOUTH WALES.

Edward Hamilton, Esq.
Sir Daniel Cooper.
Jas. Macarthur, Esq.

Alex. Stuart, Esq.
W. Sedgwick S. Cowper, Esq.

QUEENSLAND.

M. H. Marsh, Esq. M.P.
Arthur Hodgson, Esq.

Alfred Denison, Esq.
Henry Jordan, Esq. Secretary.

VICTORIA.

Sir Edmund Barry. C. E. Bright, Esq.
John Geo. Knight, Esq.

SOUTH AUSTRALIA.

Sir Richard M. Macdonnell. G. S. Walters, Esq.
Alex. Laing Elder, Esq. Francis S. Dutton, Esq.

WESTERN AUSTRALIA.—*Alex. Andrews, Esq.*

TASMANIA.

Sir H. E. Fox Young, C.B. Fred. A. Du Croz, Esq.
Joseph Milligan, M.D. F.L.S. James A. Boul, Esq.

NEW ZEALAND.

John Morrison, Esq. M. Holmes, Esq.

5.—MEDITERRANEAN COLONIES.

MALTA.— *Hon. F. V. Inglott.*

6.—EASTERN COLONIES.

CEYLON.—*E. Rawdon Power, Esq.*

MAURITIUS.—*James Morris, Esq.*

HONG KONG.—*Patrick Campbell, Esq.*

MEDITERRANEAN PROTECTORATE.

IONIAN ISLANDS.—Drummond Wolff, Esq.

7.—MISCELLANEOUS FOREIGN STATIONS.

Manley Hopkins, Esq.

FEEJEE ISLANDS.—*London Commissioner.*

JAPAN.

Rutherford Alcock, Esq. Patrick Campbell, Esq.

SIAM.—P. L. Simmonds, Esq., Deputy-Superintendent of Colonial Departments at the Exhibition.

At 1 o'clock the Special International Representatives of all the principal Foreign Countries were met by Her Majesty's Commissioners for the Exhibition of 1862, at the North Entrance to the Horticultural Gardens (made part of the Exhibition for the day), whence they proceeded to the Däis in the Gardens, and, after a short address of welcome by Earl Granville, a Report on the work of the Juries was delivered by the Right Hon. Lord Taunton from the Council of Chairmen—as follows:

REPORT OF THE COUNCIL OF CHAIRMEN ON THE WORK OF THE JURIES.

The work of the several Juries having been brought to a termination, it becomes the duty of the Council of Chairmen to explain the manner in which the Juries were constituted, and the result of their labours.

The Juries consisted of English and Foreign members in varying proportions. The English Jurors were in the first place nominated by exhibitors, and these nominations having been carefully considered, Her Majesty's Commissioners invariably appointed such persons as appeared to be named by the general agreement of a trade or district. In cases where the nominations were not made on a common understanding, the Royal Commissioners were guided in their choice by the number of votes given to particular individuals, and, in some instances, by the desire expressed by exhibitors that the Commissioners should themselves select persons possessing the necessary qualifications.

The British Colonies were represented by Jurors recommended by the several Colonial Commissioners.

Foreign nations taking part in the Exhibition had a right to nominate one Juror for every class in which they were represented by twenty exhibitors, and for every section of a class in which they had fifteen exhibitors. As an alternative, each nation had a certain number of Jurors allotted to it, in proportion to the space which it occupied in the building, and several countries accepted this alternative. Her Majesty's Commissioners, without fixing any arbitrary proportion between Foreign and English Jurors, appointed as many of the latter to each Jury as the experience of past Exhibitions showed to be necessary for its efficiency.

The Juries were sixty-five in number, grouped so as to form thirty-six classes or Head Juries corresponding to the thirty-six industrial classes under which the objects are arranged in the Exhibition. Each of these Head Juries, when subdivided into sections, acted as a united body for the confirmation of awards. Before, however, these awards were considered final, they were brought before and received the sanction of a Council, consisting of the Chairmen of the thirty-six Head Juries. The Chairmen, forming the Council which regulated the affairs of the Juries, were nominated by Her Majesty's Commissioners from the Jurors of different nations, a number being allotted to each country relatively to the space assigned to it in the building. The Council was presided over by a Chairman appointed by Her Majesty's Commissioners.

Her Majesty's Commissioners decided that only one description of Medal should be awarded by the Juries. This decision considerably facilitated their labours, as it became necessary only to reward excellence wherever it was found, without reference to competition between exhibitors. As the work of the Juries advanced, it was ascertained that many articles possessed excellence of a kind which deserved a special mention, without, however, entitling them to a Medal; and although it involved some departure from the principle that had been originally laid down, yet the Council of Chairmen acceded to the wish of the Juries, and permitted such cases to be classed and published under the title of " Honourable Mentions."

The Jurors and their associates engaged in examining the objects of the Exhibition amounted to 615 persons, of whom 287 were Foreigners, and 328 English. They are men of high social, scientific, and industrial position, drawn from nearly every civilized country in the world. Their labours have occupied two months, and have been of the most arduous description, as they had to examine the objects displayed by at least 25,000 exhibitors. It can scarcely be expected that none of the articles exhibited have escaped their attention. In a few instances the delay of arrival or of arrangement has rendered it impossible for the Juries to examine every article now within the building; while, in other cases, errors in classification have rendered it doubtful to which of the Juries the duty of examining some particular object should fall. Every effort, however, has been made to conquer these obstacles, and the omissions, if any, must be very few in number, and are not owing to the want of attention of the Juries or of the officers engaged in facilitating their work.

The number of Medals voted by the Juries amount to nearly 7,000, and the Honourable Mentions to about 5,300. The proportion of awards to exhibitors is greater than in the International Exhibition of 1851, but less than in that of 1855.

Notwithstanding the varied nationalities represented in the Juries, it is gratifying to record that the. utmost harmony has prevailed during the whole time that the Jurors have been associated in their labours. The mutual dependence and intimate alliance between the industries of the world have been illustrated by the zealous and impartial efforts of the Jurors of different nations to recognise and reward the merit displayed in the exhibitions of their industrial competitors.

We are glad to observe that the state of industry, as shown in the International Exhibition, gives evidence of a singularly active and healthy progress throughout the civilized world; for while we find every nation searching for new raw materials or utilizing products hitherto considered as waste, we are struck especially with the vast improvement in the machinery employed to adapt them to industrial purposes, as well as with the applications of science and with the great and successful attention which is now given to all the arts necessary to gratify our taste and sense of beauty.

We cannot conclude this Report without expressing our obligations to Dr. Lyon Playfair, the Special Commissioner for Juries, for the constant and intelligent assistance which he has rendered to us throughout our labours, as well as to the Deputy Commissioners and Secretary who have acted under his direction, and have afforded efficient aid to the several Juries during their inquiries.

TAUNTON,
President of the Council.

The Duke of Cambridge having replied, and the other preliminary ceremonies, as set forth in the Official programme, being concluded, a procession was formed, which included The Duke of Cambridge, The Pasha of Egypt, and other Special International Representatives, Her Majesty's Commissioners for Exhibition of 1862, Her Majesty's Ministers, The Commissioners for Exhibition of 1851, The Lord Mayor of London and Suite, The Jurors, &c. &c., and, entering by the Eastern Annexe, passed along towards the appointed Stations within the Building.

On the arrival of the Procession at the Victoria Trophy, where the Colonial Commissioners were assembled, His Royal Highness handed to the Chairman of each a handsomely-bound book of 459 pages, containing a list of the Awards of " Medals " and " Honorable Mentions " assigned to Exhibitors of the various countries, British, Colonial, and Foreign, whose natural products, manufactures, and works of art were displayed in the Exhibition of 1862.

The *Colonies* gained, in all, 437 *Medals,* and 515 *Honourable Mentions,* as will be seen by the accompanying tabular statement:—

TABLE OF COLONIAL EXHIBITORS AND OF MEDALS AND HONORABLE MENTIONS AWARDED.

	NO. EXHIBITORS.	MEDALS.	HON. MENTIONS.
Indian Empire	532	59	147
North American Colonies:—			
Canada	104	63	20
Nova Scotia.	65	14	10
New Brunswick . . .	36	5	9
Newfoundland	22	4	1
Prince Edward Island .		3	
Vancouver	6	1	
Bermuda		1	4
Columbia	21	1	1
Jamaica	216	57	68
Other West Indian Isles . .		30	15
Natal		12	8
New South Wales	469	41	34
South Australia	77	18	18
West Australia	68	4	11
Victoria	542	66	85
Queensland	93	13	18
Tasmania	158	20	26
New Zealand	115	5	10
Ceylon	41	9	7
Mauritius	25	4	5
Malta and other Stations . .		7	9

Of the 92 Medals and 49 Honourable Mentions awarded to the North American Colonies, there were assigned to Canada upwards of 60 Medals and 29 Honourable Mentions.

The whole number of Canadian Exhibitors may be set down as 194. Of Specimens of Mineral Products from Canada there were 37 exhibitors, by whom materials from upwards of 200 different localities were displayed, and of whom 36 were private individuals, or incorporated companies,—for about *three-fourths* of the mineral products on exhibition in the Canadian Court were entered in the name of "The Geological Survey" of the Province, which appears as *one* of the 37 exhibitors.

It is but just, as regards Canada, to state that while there is no reason to be dissatisfied with the number of Medals and Honourable Mentions assigned to her, yet it has been felt and expressed by numerous Canadian visitors to the Exhibition that the display of products was by no means so extensive, so varied, or so generally excellent as to do full justice to the country. From many parts, both in the Eastern and Western Districts, there were no specimens whatever of natural products or manufactures. The manufactures of the Eastern Townships in particular were not displayed in a single instance. But it is to be borne in mind that although the utmost was done with the Canadian collection to exhibit it to the best advantage, the Commissioners in London could not make up for all deficiencies growing out of the smallness of the means placed at their disposal, or for such defects as sprung from delay in commencing preparations in Canada. It was felt that at least a whole year should have been allotted to the work of preparation. The products displayed were virtually got together during the space from December to February, and despatched to England in March. It is easy to see that various products prepared in Canada in the winter season are not necessarily the best of their kind that the country affords—not to name the greater difficulties encountered in procuring them. The Provincial geological collection sufficed in part to prevent defects so far as one great class of industrial objects and pursuits are concerned, and it was admitted by all that ample justice was, under the circumstances, done to that branch.

Upon the whole, however, notwithstanding the deficiencies obvious to persons acquainted with the capabilities of Canada at this day, the favourably expressed opinions of English and Foreign visitors to the " Canadian Court," and the results generally of the Exhibition cannot but prove gratifying to the Province at large.

The display of articles in the Canadian Court at the Exhibition was much facilitated through the active and most obliging services of the curator, Wm. Dixon, Esq., formerly of Toronto, in Canada West. The value of this gentleman's constant attendance in the office can scarcely be overrated on account of his ever-ready and lucid explanations in reply to the interrogatories of innumerable visitors to the Court.

In conclusion, we must not omit to refer to the obligations which Canada, in common with the Colonies at large, lies under on this important occasion to *Dr. Lindley*, the eminent botanist, Superintendent of the Colonial Departments at the Exhibition, as well as to his able deputy *P. L. Simmonds, Esq.* These gentlemen were indefatigable in the discharge of their various onerous duties, and in acts of courtesy to the Colonial Commissioners and Exhibitors. The writer has, therefore, much pleasure in appending the following letters expressive of the obligations here adverted to:—

Copy of Letter of the Duke of Newcastle to Dr. Lindley respecting the Colonial Departments at the International Exhibition.

Downing Street, 4th June, 1862.

MY DEAR DR. LINDLEY,

Now that the Colonial Department of the International Exhibition is very nearly complete, I must express to you, first, my thanks for the trouble you took in showing me the various productions, and, next, my extreme admiration of the spirited and successful manner in which the Colonies, with scarcely an exception, have responded to the invitation of the Commissioners to send specimens of their natural products and their industry for the information and, I may well add, the instruction of the Nations of Europe.

It is impossible that such a display of what the Colonial portions of the British Empire can produce should be without a very material influence upon the future prospects and prosperity of each of them. In gold and other metals, in cereal produce, in timber, in wool, above all in cotton, the visitors of the Exhibition will find the English Colonies eclipsing all competitors, and I am much mistaken if Foreigners will not find in the department allotted to them more to excite their admiration and wonder than in the more showy and artistic displays, which do so much credit to the taste, energy, and manufacturing power of the mother country.

I assure you that not only officially but individually I am delighted at the position before the world which the Colonies have assumed in the Exhibition.

I am, my dear Dr. Lindley,

Yours very sincerely,

NEWCASTLE.

Copy of a Letter addressed by the Canadian Commissioners to Dr. Lindley.

Canadian Department, Exhibition Building,
July 14th, 1862.

DEAR DR. LINDLEY,

The Canadian Commission here having been reorganized in consequence of the approaching departure of some of its members, we feel that we cannot separate without tendering to you our heartiest thanks for the unwearied attention you have given to Colonial interests, and for the assiduous labour you have devoted to the discharge of the onerous duties imposed on you as Colonial Superintendent.

The governments and people of the several Colonies represented here owe you a debt of gratitude for what you have done in their behalf on this occasion, as on that of the first great International Exhibition, to which on behalf of Canada we desire to give expression. We consider ourselves fortunate in having been brought into official connection with a gentleman who so thoroughly understands and appreciates the great resources of the Colonial Empire.

Wishing you many happy years in which to enjoy the general esteem, and the distinction in the scientific world which you have so fairly won,

We remain, dear Dr. Lindley,

Your very obedient servants,

W. E. LOGAN,
J. HURLBURT,
B. CHAMBERLIN,
HENRY H. MILES.

John Lindley, Esq., M.D., F.R.S.
&c. &c.

————————

Copy of Dr. Lindley's Reply.

August 4th, 1862.

MY DEAR SIR,

The flattering letter you have been so kind as to send me on the part of the Canadian Commission demands my warm acknowledgments. Could anything add to the satisfaction of feeling that one has done one's best to execute faithfully a public duty it is the knowledge that the endeavour is appreciated by those best able to form a correct judgment. I must, however, observe that nothing which I may have done would have been of value to Canada in the absence of the admirably-directed and untiring exertions of yourself and your brother Commissioners.

Pray do me the favour to convey to them the assurance that I feel most sensibly the extremely kind manner in which they and yourself have done the honour to address me.

I am, yours very sincerely,

JOHN LINDLEY.

B. Chamberlin, Esq.,
Secretary, Canadian Commissioners.

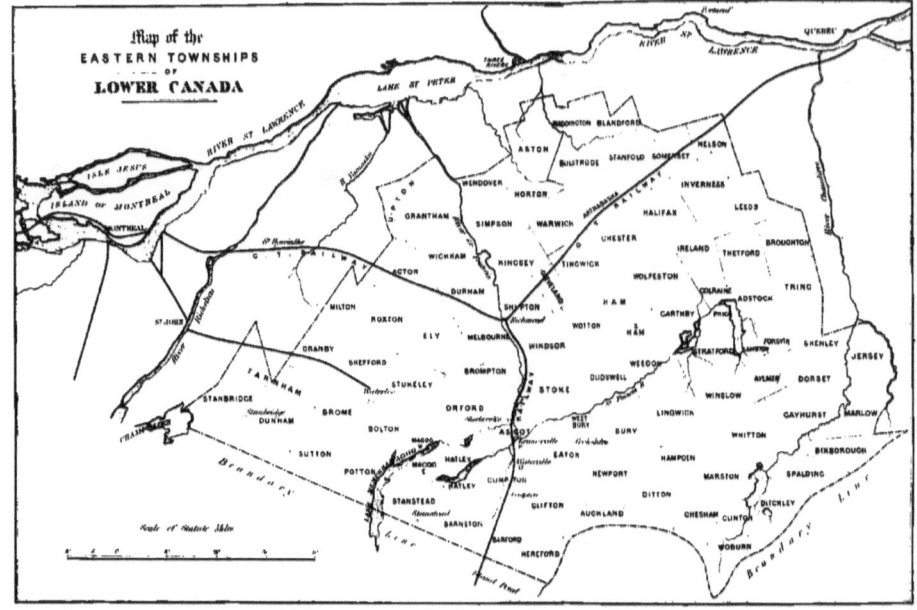

EASTERN TOWNSHIPS OF LOWER CANADA.

CHAPTER I.

INTRODUCTION—OF CANADA GENERALLY.

Colonists sojourning in England are sometimes amazed at the vague-ness of the knowledge possessed by the English public on subjects relating to their own possessions abroad.

It might of course be expected that people generally would be ill-informed about the more recently founded colonies—but it is remarkable that such should be the case with respect to those which have cost England dear for their acquisition, defence, and maintenance, and which, in the increase of their population, the development of their internal resources, and their progress in self-government and the arts of life generally, are beginning to afford indications of fitness to assume, at no distant day, the position of independent nations.

Not to speak of the several communities of British North America, but confining the attention to Canada alone, it cannot but be a subject, both of regret and of surprise, that the value of this great province, as an integral portion of the British Empire, should be so imperfectly realized here. Every person who is really acquainted with Canada, and who is not under the influence of prejudice or party spirit, knows that this is the case. Whether Colonist or not, no man can doubt it; one has only to refer to the course of current events, the debates in Parliament, the editorials of leading newspapers, and the tone of conversation out of doors.

Under these circumstances, the writer of the following notice, although his aim is to present information about a mere section of Canada, finds it necessary to his purpose to begin by referring to the country at large, seeing that it is in name alone really known to the majority of the British public.

Let us understand, at the outset, that the past progress of the Province, its value and future prospects, can be far more distinctly apprehended through statements made in the *American House of Congress* than through what transpires from the lips of members of our own British Parliament. In Reports prepared by American Committees of the House of Repre-sentatives all facts of material importance relative to Canada are pro-minently set forth for the information of their own people; all the hitherto discovered natural resources, peculiar advantages of position with respect to contiguous territory, progress achieved in past years, and estimates of what may be looked for in future, are brought out with so much clear-ness and force that no man can rise from the perusal of those Reports without reflecting that, were they not framed expressly in view of dealing with certain commercial treaties now subsisting between the United States and the Province, the Americans must be contemplating the arrival of that period when John Bull's apathy about his foreign possessions should attain its climax, and when that ancient Province should be cast adrift on the world.

After duly placing on record "that Canada consists chiefly of a vast projection into the territory of the United States—that it possesses a coast of nearly 1000 miles on the river and gulf of St. Lawrence, where fisheries of cod, herring, mackerel, and salmon, are carried on successfully, in addition to the valuable fisheries in its lakes—that it is rich in metallic ores and the resources of its forests—that its territory is peculiarly favourable to the growth of wheat, barley, and other cereals," these Reports present two remarkable statements worthy of the attention of every thoughtful well-wisher of the British Empire. "The British possessions on this continent have now a population nearly equal in number to that of our Union at the time of its origin, and nearly twice as large as that of the seven originally seceding states, sprung from the two great rival nations of the Old World," and "during the last quarter of a century the population of Canada has increased more than fourfold, from 582,000 to 2,500,000; and it is computed that Canada alone, if her past and present rate of increase is continued, will have *twenty millions* of inhabitants at the end of this present century, numerically exceeding the population of Great Britain when this century began."

The foregoing extracts at least prove that our American rivals do not regard the "Canadas" with any feeling akin to contempt, while the statements embody facts which the truly loyal Canadian people would earnestly desire their fellow subjects in England to give them some credit for whenever partizanship at home takes the form of undervaluing the colonies, or of menacing them with the withdrawal of British military protection.

Lying between the meridians of about 65° and 90° west, and, for the most part, between the parallels of 43° and 53° of north latitude, Canada is within ten or eleven days' sail of the principal English and Irish sea-ports. It is possible however, on occasions of importance, for intercommunication to take place in about *six days* through the aid of telegraphic connection between England and Queenstown or Londonderry on this side of the Atlantic and between Belleisle and Quebec on the other. In fact, so far as distance is concerned, Canada may now be held to be virtually no further off from the British Isles than Scotland or Ireland were from the Metropolis seventy or eighty years back.

Nor has the advancement of the country been confined solely to the discovery and development of natural resources. Conjointly with these and the increase of population noticed in the American Reports, very great progress has been accomplished in all that goes to constitute foundations for future national existence. Even if comparison be made with the

United States themselves there has been no greater improvement during any decade of their wonderful history up to the breaking out of their civil war than that witnessed in Canada during the ten years terminating in 1861. Very important and for a long time embarrassing questions, relating to municipal and political privileges, religion, education, administration of the law, and the abolition of feudal tenure, have been satisfactorily adjusted. Nor can there be any reasonable doubt but that all remaining hindrances to the political and social welfare of the people of Canada will in due time be surmounted.

From the narratives of emigrants and visitors issued twenty years ago, people in England who have not looked further into the matter can form no just estimate of the facilities for conducting all the internal business of the country. Long journeys of 400 and 500 miles can now be performed by rail with a degree of comfort, speed, and punctuality not surpassed in any country of Europe. Indeed there are at least 2000 miles of railroad communication in operation in Canada alone. At the same time there is scarcely any settled locality in the Province from which the inhabitants do not enjoy perfectly easy access to other parts, and from which, whether travelling for pleasure or for business, they cannot readily pass to any leading place in the American Union or to the sea-board for the purpose of embarking for Europe.

The gigantic river St. Lawrence, expanding in the interior into five immense lakes or inland seas, supplies, at least during seven or eight months of the year, the requisites of cheap water communication through the entire length of the country. Through this natural channel vast stores of grain and provisions are transmitted from the west to the ports of Montreal and Quebec, and, as may be conceived, while we are speaking of a water route of thousands of miles, the lumber and other products of the forests and soil of Canada, find their way to the same outlets through numerous considerable rivers, by which the regions lying north and south of the St. Lawrence are drained into that river. Impediments to navigation at several points above Montreal are surmounted by means of a magnificent system of canals, whose construction, though costly, was indispensable for procuring a free communication between the ocean and the Lake regions, by means of steamers and sailing vessels.

A very common objection to Canada is stated to be its rigorous climate. It would be easy to demonstrate to the satisfaction of every candid mind that the objection is without any real foundation. The inhabitants themselves do not find their ordinary avocations interrupted by severe weather to an extent greater than is the case, in some form or other, in all the known countries of the world. Indeed the atmospheric irregularities of all countries under the sun are probably felt by their own inhabitants to be as objectionable (and in most cases more so) as the occasional extremes of heat and cold in Canada. The monsoons of the East, the siroccos of Italy and Spain, the whirlwinds and hurricanes of the West

c

Indies, the drenching and continuous rains of the Tropics, and even the foggy, moist atmosphere of Great Britain, might, with equal force, be cited in disparagement of regions contentedly occupied by millions of the human race. In fact, the lowness of temperature which occurs a few times between December and March is proportionably compensated by the dry, pure, and quiescent state of the air, of which the effects are healthful and exhilarating. The monotonous aspect of a vast tract covered with snow from the beginning of December to the end of March does not afflict the feelings of the Canadians as it appears to do the minds of those who quote it in England as a drawback. For then is the time for the most joyous interchange of visits of relatives and friends throughout the country, and residing separated from each other by considerable distances. While there is plenty of profitable occupation at home of various kinds, for those who have farm premises and stock to look after, the repose of nature and the excellent snow roads invite all to indulge themselves with occasional holiday trips across the country. Very few indeed are so poor that they cannot participate in such winter recreation as is afforded by a sleigh-ride; not to speak of the convenience to all, both rich and poor, wherever located, of having access to neighbouring markets over roads more smooth and comfortable than the finest turnpikes of England. In short, to the great bulk of the inhabitants of Canada the winter time is the happiest, and perhaps no greater calamity could befal them than during one winter season to have their territory denuded of snow, seeing that this at once provides them with ready and agreeable means of locomotion, and protects vegetation, preventing its temporary suspension from becoming perpetual through the destructive agency of frost. It may appear to some not a little singular in connection with what is here said about Canadian winters that the people of England should be so generally impressed with sentiments of an opposite kind. As a probable reason, we may, perhaps, attribute their origin to the narratives of the earliest visitors to British North America, followed in more recent times by the accounts of trials endured by the earlier settlers and emigrants, who went ill-prepared to encounter any considerable changes of climate. The misapprehensions existing on the subject have thus come down as an established tradition to the present time. They operate, it is feared, in preventing the most ancient and nearest colonies from receiving speedily such accessions of emigrants as are alone needed to place them on a footing of permanent prosperity. Some persons, indeed, emigrate who are unfitted to prosper either at home or abroad, and such are too ready to ascribe to causes external, and beyond their control, their own want of success. It may be added, that as yet colonial life in any part of the world is necessarily accompanied with the experience of a state of things different from that which subsists in the oldest and most civilized countries ; so that those who are only fitted to exist amidst the superabundant requirements of elegant life in England and France, usually do, when they come to Canada, complain of the unexpected high and low temperatures that sometimes occur there. But, so far as respects people in general and the ordinary avocations of agricultural, professional, and even refined life and intercourse, there is no substantial reason for asserting that the climate of Canada unfits it for becoming the seat of a numerous, prosperous, and contented people. On the contrary, various facts, which will present themselves in a more advanced part of this notice, amply suffice to disprove the objections commonly raised on that score.

It is understood that the territory of Canada embraces a surface of about 350,000 square miles. Her present population may be stated at about 2,600,000, having under actual cultivation upwards of 10,000,000 of acres of land. Of the whole population, about 2,250,000 may be reckoned as belonging to the rural districts, the remainder, being about one-tenth of the whole, living in the towns, and constituting the population of the seven principal cities, Quebec, Montreal, Ottawa, Kingston, Toronto, Hamilton, and London. The cities of Montreal and Quebec in Canada East are by far the most populous in Canada; and the former is progressing in wealth and every substantial advantage, at a rate of which there are few parallels in the whole world. The population of Montreal probably exceeds 100,000, while that of Quebec, which was only 40,000 in 1851, has now attained to between 60,000 and 70,000.

The cash value of all the farms and live stock of the rural population may be set down at upwards of £110,000,000 sterling.

When we reflect that this large amount of property is owned by people who for the most part, either themselves or their immediate predecessors, took little or nothing with them into their adopted country—that they want for scarcely any single blessing, whether political, municipal, spiritual, educational, or social, that appertains to the prosperous portions of any civilized community elsewhere—that throughout Canada a man with his family can retire to rest at night with a conviction that when morning comes again he will rise secure in the possession of what belonged to him the day before, and in the same perfect liberty of speech and action—we cannot refrain from wondering that so many thousands of families, constituting the surplus population of Great Britain and other crowded European countries should unnecessarily continue to live in comparative scarcity and anxiety about their daily wants.

It is only, however, by descending to actual details that any exposition of Canadian resources can be made clearly intelligible to those for whose benefit chiefly it is intended—besides which descriptions applicable to different parts of the country would necessarily vary much.

The writer, therefore, does not conceive that there is occasion to devote more space to remarks about the colony at large, but that it will be more useful to confine himself chiefly to a brief description of that important section, with the circumstances of which, by personal experience, he is best acquainted.

CHAPTER II.

THE EASTERN TOWNSHIPS.

GEOGRAPHICAL POSITION AND NATURAL FEATURES—EARLIEST SETTLERS
—POPULATION AND OCCUPATIONS OF THE INHABITANTS—COMPARA-
TIVE REFERENCE TO THE UNITED STATES AND NEW SETTLEMENTS IN
THE FAR WEST—POLITICAL AND MUNICIPAL PRIVILEGES—TAXATION.

THE earliest European settlements in Canada were distributed in the
vicinity of the Gulf and River St. Lawrence, more especially where the
cities of Quebec and Montreal now stand, and in the splendid and extensive valley of that great river. In this valley, to the south of the St.
Lawrence, the most prosperous settlements were permanently established,
and there, to this day, the great bulk of their descendants flourish, constituting the majority of the *French Canadian* population of Lower Canada.

Further south of the St. Lawrence, beyond the French settlements,
and lying eastwards of Montreal, an extensive tract is included under the
designation of "The Eastern Townships." It is a tract of about one-sixth
the size of England, if we take in all the portions of territory which is
comprehended in the Government Surveys. A full "township" should
enclose a surface of *ten miles square*, or *one hundred square miles*, and there
are between ninety and one hundred such divisions; so that the Eastern
Townships may be spoken of summarily as a region comprising nearly *six
millions of acres*.

The settling of the Eastern Townships, now occupied by what may be
called an English speaking Protestant community, may be stated to have
begun about the beginning of the present century. Many of the earlier
occupants of the territory were royalists from the neighbouring New
England States, persons of indomitable energy, who accomplished by their
self-reliance, industry, perseverance, and skill, a conquest more or less
complete, in various directions over the obstacles presented by nature.
These have for the most part passed away, after stamping deeply upon the
character both of their descendants and of the emigrants who joined them
from other parts of the world, the impress of their own enterprising and
virtuous dispositions. Through the efforts and assistance of the Government at different times in establishing roads and encouraging settlement
by grants of land, much was done; but still more credit is due to the
exertions and example of various patriotic individuals, and especially to
the officers of one of the settled institutions of the townships—The
British American Land Company—of which some account will be given in
a future page.

At the present time, as will be shewn, the occupants of the Eastern

Townships have attained to the possession of all requirements necessary to the happiness of a civilized community, and, favoured by all external circumstances, and with such accessions to their force as may reasonably be looked for in the shape of *good inhabitants*, attracted from the over-crowded populations in the old world, they will undoubtedly exercise a great influence upon the future destinies of Canada. In order to accelerate the results hinted at, nothing more seems to be needed than to make known in the proper quarters, their peculiar physical and other ad-vantages.

The appended Map indicates the relative positions of the several Townships, and the situation of the entire tract with respect to Quebec and Montreal and the adjoining territory of the United States. The most contiguous of the States are those of Maine, New Hampshire, Ver-mont, and New York.

The map also shews the courses and positions of several principal rivers. The Chaudiere eastwards, the St. Francis pursuing a circuitous route through the midst of the Townships, the Yamaska and the Richelieu to the west—all pursuing a northerly course and emptying into the St. Lawrence. The surface is everywhere intersected by other smaller streams, running for the most part into those which have been already named, and which, with many rivulets, beautiful lakes, and innumerable springs of the purest water gushing out of the ground, render the Eastern Townships one of the most picturesque and best-watered regions in North America. It is this circumstance—the abundance of running water with the diversified cha-racter of the scenery and surface throughout the Eastern Townships—conjoined with excellence of soil for agricultural purposes, that, physically speaking, confers so great an advantage upon them over all the rich alluvial tracts in the far West, which have of late years been so sedulously held up to view for emigration from the old world.

The population of the Eastern Townships in the year 1862 may be stated at about 200,000. A great number of them are as yet but very sparsely inhabited. The most populous, as well as those longest settled, and most advanced, are the townships of Orford and Ascot, Compton, Eaton, Mel-bourne, Shipton, and upwards of twenty other townships included in the counties of Stanstead, Missisquoi, and Shefford. Taking the whole of the townships together, as appears from the results of the late census, the average increase of population in ten years has been about *fifty per cent*. It must be understood, however, that the great apparent increase which has occurred in those most recently occupied has arisen chiefly from the encouragement given to many families to remove into the new townships from the older settlements near the St. Lawrence.

The greater part of the inhabitants of the townships are engaged in agriculture. The agricultural capabilities will receive a more particular notice further on. But although, as yet, the manufacturing portion of the population is small, it is believed, not even excepting the State of Massachusetts, no section of country in North America is more amply provided by nature with the fundamental requisites for establishing profitably manufactures of all kinds. Some progress has indeed been already made by the people themselves in that direction, as will be seen.

In proportion to the inhabitants, the other occupations are duly followed; Law, Medicine, Education, Commerce, engaging the services of a considerable number of persons. It may also be mentioned, in speaking of the population generally, and as a happy circumstance, when the Eastern Townships are compared with the new settlements in the far West, that they are exempt from those hideous consequences attendant upon rapid growth in population and material prosperity, unaccompanied by a regard for the observance of the Sabbath, and provision for spiritual interests. A numerous and truly efficient body of clergy and ministers of religion of various Christian denominations live amongst the people, stationed at or near all the principal settlements in the district.

In fact it has been for many years past too much the fashion to present to the minds of intending emigrants from over populous localities in Europe, the claims of those parts of North America which are situated, in many respects, beyond the confines of civilization. More remote from the great markets of the world, those distant, though fertile regions are known to be less healthy for settlers—far less fitted for becoming the seats of manufacturing as well as agricultural communities, far less amply stocked by nature with valuable timber and building materials, and, finally, those who have been attracted thither by glowing accounts of fertility which it would be idle to claim in favour of the more easterly British provinces, have commonly left behind them nearly all the advantages of civilized life. Many have returned; many more would return, if it were in their power to do so, from parts where money is borrowed with avidity at fifteen to twenty per cent. interest, and where the crops of grain when raised cannot be profitably sold, and have even been employed as fuel because they could not endure the cost of transport by rail or steamboat. In fact, the inhabitants of the Eastern Townships are at the present time consuming, in the shape of flour, *at about five dollars (one sovereign)* per barrel of 196lbs., wheat raised in the Western Country, and offered for that moderate price at their doors. Grain which has been transported so far for consumption, and which has been handled perhaps two or three times in its progress, cannot, as a matter of course, after expenses for storage, and the intermediate profit of agents and vendors, realize much to the parties chiefly interested—the growers.

With the inducements offered for the introduction of more abundant capital for carrying on mining operations, for the working of the valuable deposits of marbles, soapstone, and other minerals, and for turning to account in various manufactures the immense amount of water power available within the limits of the Townships, it may be hoped, as has been already said, that it is only necessary to diffuse in the right quarters, reliable information about their resources, in order to attract a more just share of the attention of emigrants from the British isles.

Of persons dependent on agriculture alone, at least 20,000 additional families possessing small capitals, and industriously disposed, might at once locate themselves, and enter upon a career of comfort and usefulness which, in England or Scotland, as small farmers, they can have no reasonable prospect of attaining. For agriculturalists in a larger way, and possessing capitals from £1000 and upwards, there is no section of country in North America which holds out a more certain prospect of success. And, as regards families with moderate independent incomes, to whom, in Great Britain, the present is so commonly embittered by thinking of the future, and by the feeling that while they have quite enough to live upon economically, they are quite unable to educate and start in life their children according to their wishes, a settlement in the Eastern Townships would at once give a new and agreeable turn to their prospects, relieving their minds immediately of all doubt and embarrassment.

In view of considerable accessions to the existing population of the Townships, it may be stated that even in North America there are tracts of country less well fitted for agricultural occupations, less extensive, and at least not better provided with the natural requisites for establishing works and manufactures, which are found to have space for a very much larger number of inhabitants. Several of the States of the American Union might be cited as examples; but it will be enough to refer to the New England State, Massachusetts. Although settled at an early period, this State is smaller than the territory of the Eastern Townships; its soil is for the most part inferior. Its manufacturing capabilities have been industriously promoted, and its people display at all times a wonderful amount of energy of character, so that as a distinct community they exercise a very considerable influence upon the national proceedings. The number of its inhabitants is about 1,250,000, and will doubtless far exceed that in future years. If we make fair allowance for the better soil of the Eastern Townships, for their mineral and forest resources, and for their equal, if not greater natural facilities for manufactures, it becomes difficult to see why they also may not comfortably accommodate upwards of *two millions* of people. The parallel here suggested might appear over-strained, if it were not mentioned that the noble harbour of Portland, virtually a Canadian sea-port, and the natural outlet of the Grand Trunk Railway passing through the Townships, from which it can be reached in a few hours, is decidedly superior, in natural fitness for all commercial purposes, to the harbour of Boston. Another reason favouring the same inference is the immediate connection by railway between the Townships and each of our own cities and sea-ports, Quebec and Montreal. Nor should we omit all allusion, in this case, to our own form of government, more reliably permanent, and better fitted to the genius of the British colonists than that of their republican neighbours. The people of the

Townships, while they enjoy perfect political freedom, derive an immense advantage from the absence of those perpetually recurring local, state and national elections (with accompanying changes of office-bearers) by which the whole of the United States are afflicted, and the minds of their inhabitants kept in an almost constant state of turmoil.

It is proper in this place to say a few more words respecting the political and municipal advantages enjoyed by the inhabitants of the Eastern Townships, and we shall conclude the chapter with a statement of the amount of taxation to which they are subjected.

Every man who comes from Great Britain to the Townships, retains all the privileges of a British subject, and a foreigner becomes naturalized after residing continuously for three years, on taking the oath of allegiance and residence. The possession of real estate worth £5 sterling a-year, or payment of an annual rent of £5, qualifies to vote for a representative in each branch of the Provincial Legislature—the Legislative Assembly and the Legislative Council.

As representing and elected by the whole people of Canada, 130 members are returned to the former, or Lower House of Parliament, and 48 to the Upper.

The Electoral Districts of Canada East are such that the Eastern Townships are virtually represented in Parliament by fourteen members in the Assembly, and five members in the Council, as portions of the Townships are in some cases included in contiguous territory.

The right of petition is freely enjoyed—petitions being addressed, conformably to certain simple formalities, to the Sovereign (represented by the Governor-General), and to each of the two Houses. The Session of Parliament usually begins in the winter time, about February, and continues three or four months. Every man who is a householder, or resident possessor of real estate, votes in the election of seven *Municipal Councillors* for the Township in which he resides, by whom one member, selected from amongst themselves, is appointed *Warden*, who acts as Chairman of the body, and represents his own Township in the *County Council.*

By these Town and County Councils, acting in conformity with their respective by-laws, all the local affairs are regulated—such as the imposition and collection of the taxes for constructing and maintaining roads, bridges, schools, proceedings of agricultural societies, &c.

The powers of the Town and County Councils are prescribed by the laws of the land, as set forth in Acts of the Provincial Legislature.

From what has been stated it will be seen that the inhabitants of the Townships enjoy all the privileges of representation in Parliament and of local self-government.

On the important subject of *Taxation,* it may be added, that the indirect taxes, paid by the people on articles of consumption, are imposed by the Legislature for the sole purpose of meeting the expenses of the public service and the just claims of the public creditor; and the matter is so adjusted that the burden falls lightest upon those classes who are least able to bear it. The local taxation, established from time to time by the Municipal Councils, is conducted on similar principles, and is freely open to the supervision of the parties principally concerned, and to correction in case of any inadvertence or inequality. But, in fact, the taxes are very small compared with the ability to pay them, while the prices of food and all the necessaries of life admit of a man's living comfortably on what in England would be considered a very insignificant income.

In cases of cleared land rented, although this is not very common in the Eastern Townships, a man in England would pay from £2. 10s. to £4 per acre annually, for land of less value than he could rent in the Townships for 15s, taxes inclusive.

CHAPTER III.

CAPITAL TOWN, AND OTHER TOWNS AND VILLAGES OF THE EASTERN TOWNSHIPS.

THE capital of the Eastern Townships is *Sherbrooke*, a town which for electoral purposes has between 6000 and 7000 inhabitants. It occupies both banks of the river Magog at its confluence with the river St. Francis. The former river, after leaving the lake, called Little Magog, a few miles above Sherbrooke, descends in a rapid stream towards its junction with the St. Francis, into which it rushes tumultuously after a succession of falls, thus creating an amount of water-power which, associated with the other natural advantages of situation, will, it is believed, render it the principal seat of manufactures in Lower Canada. The town also extends to the opposite bank of the St. Francis, the communications across both the rivers being maintained by substantial bridges.

It is represented in the Provincial Parliament by one member. The principal Courts of Law of the Townships are held here, and it is the chief way-station of the Grand Trunk Railroad leading from Montreal and Quebec to Portland. Various manufactures are prosecuted; there being, besides iron foundries and mechanics' work-shops, a woollen factory, paper mill, pail and tub factory, machine factories, grist and saw mills. A very well supplied market for provisions and all kinds of country produce is held twice a week, in addition to the monthly *Cattle Fairs*, established last year by the officers of the Land Company, to the great benefit of the district. The mails arrive and depart twice daily. Various chartered Companies have their head-quarters or branch offices in the town; among which may be named The Eastern Townships Bank, The City Bank of Montreal, The British American Land Company, The Mutual, and several other Fire and Life Assurance Companies.

There are two local newspapers—the *Sherbrooke Gazette*, which has a large circulation in the Townships and elsewhere, and has now been conducted by its present editor and proprietor, with remarkable ability for about twenty-five years; and the *Sherbrooke Leader*, a paper recently established, and issued twice a week.

The new Town Hall, of which a cut is given, with accommodations in the open space and sheds underneath, is built of brick, and adds greatly to the substantial appearance of the town. Of other public buildings and places of worship, St. Peter's Episcopal Church, the Roman Catholic Church, the Congregationalists', Methodists', and the buildings recently built for schools, are all handsome structures, erected at considerable cost, of brick and stone, and remarkable for their appropriateness of design and architecture.

The town is abundantly supplied with shops and stores, where every necessary and convenience of life can be procured—the old system of long credits and high charges, formerly so great a drawback to the country, being now discountenanced by all the principal business men, who, it may be added, are, as a body, distinguished for their integrity and fair-dealing.

The medical and legal professions are represented by gentlemen of the highest order of ability in their respective callings, and of whom it is not too much to say that any where, even in the principal towns in England, they would necessarily command the respect and confidence of the people.

There is as yet no local infirmary or hospital. The County Gaol, erected many years ago near the Court House, is larger than experience has shewn to be needed by the number of criminals, of whom seldom more than one or two of a really bad class have ever been immured at the same time.

No country town in America is better off for inns; among the principal ones may be named the Magog House, conducted by Mr. Cheney, the Hotel of Mr. H. Cameron in Factory Street, that of Mr. C. Cameron in Wellington Street, and Mr. Boote's Hotel advantageously situated close to the Railroad Station. In these inns the sojourner can procure very comfortable entertainment; the charges are quite moderate, and, what is usually of equal consequence to strangers, one meets with the utmost civility and even kindness.

There are many handsome private residences, both of wood and of brick, in and around Sherbrooke; we may instance, on the north side, those of the Rev. C. R. Reid, Sheriff Bowen, and Mr. Clarke; and within the town, those of Dr. Johnstone, Dr. Brooks, Mr. Sanborn, the late member for the county of Compton, Mr. Walton, Dr. Worthington, Mr. Robertson on the bank of the Magog, and, on the street leading southwards, the

house of the mayor, J. G. Robertson, Esq. The Hon. A. T. Galt, the Town member of Parliament and late Finance Minister of Canada, also resides in Sherbrooke, as well as Mr. Henneker, the Chief Commissioner of the British American Land Company, the Hon. Hollis Smith, the elected member for the Wellington district to the Upper House of the Provincial Legislature, and the Hon. Mr. Justice Short.

Sherbrooke is situated in about 71° 55' west longitude and 45° 23' north latitude.

It would be impracticable to furnish here a full description of each of the numerous smaller towns and villages scattered through the Eastern Townships. For the most part they are situated near to the rivers and small streams, so plentiful throughout the region, and there are very few indeed so placed as not to have, in addition to grist mills, structures with machinery erected for the purpose of applying, at least on a small scale, the abundant water-power.

One universal characteristic strikes the eye of a visitor to the Townships. Every village has its church or other place of worship, its neat academy and school-house, and its one or two blacksmith's forges. The contiguous country is almost always beautiful and picturesque, and there is no greater treat to a lover of fine scenery than to drive along the roads leading from one village to another. In the county of Compton we may mention the villages of *Lennoxville* (more particularly described in the appended letters), *Huntingville, Waterville, Compton, Eaton Corner, Cookshire, Bury,* and *Lingwick.*

Huntingville, on the banks of the Salmon River, is remarkable for its tannery and the long established and excellent grist and saw-mills, equipped in the most perfect manner by their enterprising proprietor, Mr. Mallory.

Further south, at *Waterville,* about five miles from Lennoxville, on the line of the railroad, rather extensive works, including Iron Foundry and various applications of machinery, have been established, chiefly through the influence and exertions of Charles Brooks, Esq., the Warden of the County and Mayor of the Township of Ascot. It has a magnificent back country and many highly cultivated farms adjacent.

The village of *Compton,* which has about 300 inhabitants, about 16 miles distant from Lennoxville, 18 from Sherbrooke, and one mile from the line of railway, is the immediate centre of a district presenting evidences of great agricultural prosperity, and the surrounding scenery is of the most beautiful description.

The other villages named are in the eastern portion of the county. *Eaton Corner* with about 250 inhabitants, is 13 miles from the line, and is a thriving place, with a daily mail from the cities, and communicating by stage with a great number of settlements in the adjacent townships.

Cookshire, the county town, is the residence of the county member of Parliament, John Henry Pope, Esq., to whose enlightened and enterprising character and liberality this portion of the country, and, indeed, the Townships at large, are deeply indebted for the promotion of their agricultural and other interests. The place stands on a site commanding one of the most beautiful and extensive views in the province. Circuit Courts are held here. It has communication daily with other neighbouring places and with the cities by stage to Lennoxville and Sherbrooke, from which latter Cookshire is distant about 16 miles. Its population is from 250 to 300.

Bury, with a population of about 120, and *Lingwick*, are the most distant villages in the county eastwards—the former 24 miles from Sherbrooke and the latter 35. The lands in their neighbourhood have attracted much attention during the last twenty years, and are thought to be equal to any in the province, and to offer very favourable prospects to settlers with small capital.

Coaticook, in the Township of Barnston, on the line of the Grand Trunk Railway, about 20 miles south of Lennoxville, is a very thriving village of three or four hundred inhabitants. It is on the river *Coaticook*, and in the vicinity of some of the principal rapids of that small river. As there is access to any amount of water-power, and the soil of the adjacent country is very rich, it is so favourably placed that it will probably become hereafter a large town. It is a port of entry, and several manufactures have been already established.

The small towns and villages in the Townships south of Compton are numerous, and each is the centre of a fine farming district where the land is highly cultivated, and much attention given to the raising of the best breeds of live stock—horses, sheep, cattle, and pigs. *Stanstead*, close to the boundary line, has a population of about 1200. It is the residence of the late Provincial Secretary, the Hon. T. L. Terrill, as also of the County Member, Albert Knight, Esq. It is the county town, and the Circuit Courts are held here. There are also the Provincial Bank, Library Association, and Mechanics' Institute, the Academy, of high local repute, several branch Insurance Offices, and good hotels, and almost every description of business is carried on.

In the same county are *Hatley* (two villages of this name, called *East* and *West* Hatley), the beautiful village of *Georgeville* and *Magog* at the outlet of Lake Memphramagog. The scenery all across the country surrounding these last named places is such as to afford the most lively satisfaction to all visitors. Near Hatley it is diversified by the presence of a considerable lake, whose margin consists, in part of bold hilly surface, and in part of cleared and richly cultivated land. Further on towards the south-west, *Georgeville*, stated to have about 300 inhabitants, is placed on the east side of the *Lake Memphramagog*, much visited of late years by tourists. The lake is about 30 miles in length, and extends across the line into the American territory. A small steamer plies on its surface during the summer season, affording, in the course of its daily run up and down the lake, a prolonged succession of views of what many pronounce to be the most picturesque and most romantically beautiful scenery in Canada. In her trip the little steamer always calls at " The Mountain House," which is simply an inn on the west side, about midway down the lake, built at the foot of an eminence called the " Owl's Head," rising abruptly from the water's edge to a height of about 2000 feet. Here, as well as at George-ville, where there are two excellent hotels, many a visitor and tourist lingers awhile every season in enjoyment of one of the richest treats to be had anywhere throughout the province. Now that the passage across the Atlantic is accomplished with such speed and facility, it is not too much to expect that summer tourists from the British Isles may ere long begin the practice of going over for the purpose of witnessing for themselves the novelty and the attractions of this whole section of country, and of viewing nature under one of its most charming aspects. Lake Memphramagog can be reached from the railroad station at Sherbrooke or Lennoxville in a journey of less than 20 miles, over good roads.

At the village *Magog*, where the water of the lake issues and forms the river of that name, there is a vast amount of water-power available, and which has been already applied to a considerable extent in various manufactures. Its population is rated at about 250.

Northwards of Sherbrooke, and in the counties of Richmond and Drummond, are several thriving small towns and villages, among which we may mention Richmond, Melbourne, Danville, Durham, and Drummond-ville, with populations of from 200 to 400. The most noted of these from their situation are Richmond and Melbourne, which are virtually one town, whose parts are connected by a covered bridge over the St. Francis river. Richmond occupies the right bank, and Melbourne the left, the united population of the two being between 700 and 800. As the Townships advance they are likely to become places of increasing importance, on account of the junction here of the Quebec, Portland, and Western branches of the Grand Trunk Railway, and from being the seat of one of the leading Township educational institutions, *St. Francis College.* The surrounding country is rich in attractions both of scenery and soil, and contains many fine farms. Drummondville is stated to have about 400 inhabitants, and Danville 300, the latter being near to the line of railroad between Quebec and Richmond. Durham is about eight miles below Melbourne, on the St. Francis, and has a population of about 220. Nearer to Sherbrooke are situated the rising settlements of Windsor and Bromp-ton Falls ; the latter remarkable for immense water-power and the great saw-mills established there, and conducted by Mr. Clarke the proprietor. These mills, being perhaps the most extensive of their kind in America, merit a more particular notice, and will be referred to further on.

The village of Dudswell is 20 miles east of Sherbrooke, and contains about 120 inhabitants. The surrounding country is very hilly and pictu-resque. There are enormous deposits of limestone and the whole region is remarkable both for the facilities of procuring the best quality of *lime* and on account of the presence of various valuable minerals. Extremely beautiful varieties of marble are found in the vicinity, and as there is abundance of water-power it is believed that the attention of capitalists will be engaged in establishing works there on an extensive scale. It is also one of the best farming tracts in the Townships.

Westwards of Sherbrooke are some of the oldest villages of the Townships, in the counties of *Shefford*, *Brome*, and *Missisquoi*. The country in these directions possesses the richest soils, and is everywhere well stocked with water-power and valuable minerals. The scenery throughout is beautiful, and in many parts romantic. For a long time the inhabitants have enjoyed the benefit of excellent roads, but more recently their communications with the city of Montreal have been vastly improved by the construction of a second township railroad, called " The Stanstead, Shefford, and Chambly Railroad," which is intended ultimately to connect with the terminus of the Passumpsic road, passing through the valley of the Connecticut to Boston in the United States. The principal villages on this line of railroad are *Waterloo*, *West Shefford*, and *Granby* in the county of Shefford, and *West Farnham* in Missisquoi.

Waterloo is a place of about 250 inhabitants, has a local newspaper, and a branch of the Eastern Townships Bank.

West Shefford is 58 miles distant from Montreal, and is situated on the pretty river Yamaska, with about 200 inhabitants. It is the residence of the Hon. A. B. Foster, elected two years since a member of the Upper House of the Provincial Parliament.

Granby in the same county, about 50 miles from Montreal, *viâ* railroad through St. John's, has between 400 and 500 inhabitants. It also has a local newspaper, and various manufactures are carried on, and is a place which probably will become very important through its situation in a fine farming country contiguous to the railroad, and the existence of copper ores understood to lie in its vicinity.

Froste Village, in Shefford, is a smaller place, of 150 inhabitants.

West Farnham, in Missisquoi County, 35 miles from Montreal, has a population of about 800. Extensive saw-mills have been carried on here for some time, and large quantities of sawn timber prepared and exported to the United States,

Frelighsburgh, *Cowansville*, *Stanbridge*, and *Dunham*, also in Missisquoi County, are considerable villages, of about 350 inhabitants in each. *Philipsburg*, in the same county, has a population of 500, and is the residence of the Hon. Philip Moore, of the Legislative Council.

Stanbridge, in the township of that name and county of Missisquoi, has about 300 inhabitants, and is the centre of one of the wealthiest farming districts. The corporation of *Eastern Townships Bank* have recently established a branch of their institution in this place.

In the county of Brome there are the villages of *Knowlton*, *Brome*, and *Mansonville*, with about 200 to 250 inhabitants each, *Brome* is the residence of the Hon. P. H. Knowlton, also a member of the Legislative Council of Canada.

In addition to the foregoing towns and villages, mentioned by name as existing in the Eastern Townships, there are numerous smaller places and settlements springing up in different parts, of which there does not seem to be occasion here to offer any particular description.

CHAPTER IV.

CLIMATE OF THE EASTERN TOWNSHIPS—AGRICULTURE—MANUFACTURING CAPABILITIES.

WE have already alluded to the long-prevailing misapprehensions respecting the climate of Canada in general. These make it difficult, in relation to any one section of the province, to procure that amount of careful attention to the facts which is necessary to enable a mere reader to acquire for himself a rational knowledge of the subject. A person's previous experience of the climate of the British Isles, as indicated by numbers expressing the *temperature, moisture,* &c., is a very poor guide in this case, and few indeed of the thousands who annually emigrate are either fitted to make correct deductions or willing to encounter the trouble this would involve. It may be added that the effects upon the feelings are usually not measurable by means of the numerical statements. A damp winter, for example, in England, may, on the whole, produce more disagreeable sensations of *cold* (with a thermometer seldom descending to ten degrees below the freezing point) than those experienced by residents in Canada, who occasionally witness a temperature 40 or 50 degrees lower down in the scale.

Under these circumstances, the writer, in presenting the following brief Summary of the Climate of the Eastern Townships, will confine himself chiefly to the statement of such facts as any general reader can found a judgment upon, without neglecting altogether to furnish the data required by those conversant with meteorology.

The chief authority at present on meteorological matters in Canada East is Dr. Smallwood, whose observatory is situated in the neighbourhood of Montreal. For ingenuity of device, fidelity of observation, and sagacity in generalising the results and deducing useful practical deductions, he is well known to scientific persons on both sides of the Atlantic. He was preceded in these pursuits by a gentleman who has long occupied a prominent position in Lower Canada, and who has been styled by Professor Smallwood himself the "Pioneer of Canadian Meteorology," now the Hon. Mr. Justice McCord, and the Chancellor of the University in the Eastern Townships. Other observers in different parts of the country have preserved records of the principal facts relating to temperature and the general state of the weather, some of which extend back more than thirty years.

From printed reports for a series of years, kindly furnished by the above-mentioned authorities, the following small table has been prepared, shewing at a glance the conditions of mean pressure, temperature, and moisture for that part of Canada, both for the whole year and for each month :—

	Mean Annual.	Jan.	Feb.	Mar.	Apr.	May.	June.	July.	Aug.	Sept.	Oct.	Nov.	Dec.
Barometer (inches) .	29.7	29·7	29·7	29.5	29·7	29.6	29·7	29·7	29·7	29·7	29·6	29·8	29·6
Thermometer (Fahr.)	42°	13¼°	17°	26¼°	40°	54¼°	64°	71¼°	63¼°	58°	46°	32°	16¼°
Humidity . . . . (Saturation, 100)		87	80	83	81	77	77	74	76	81	82	82	83

Note.—In a recent article on "Hardy Fruits in the International Exhibition," a writer in the *English Gardener's Chronicle and Agricultural Gazette* makes use of tables of temperature (slightly differing from the above) for the vicinity of Montreal, deducing the conclusion "that abundance of fruits can be successfully grown in *Upper* Canada ;" but, in fact, the deduction, so far as reference to tables of temperature is concerned, should have been made for Canada generally, including Eastern Sections, where, as is well known, most of the productions named are found in perfection, especially apples, plums, cherries, and most of the smaller fruits grown in gardens, or met with in a wild state.

In the "Colonization Circular," No. 21, issued in 1862 by Her Majesty's Emigration Commissioners, it is stated at page 95 that the *mean range* of the thermometer, *from observations taken for one year* in Eastern Canada is 77½° for three summer months, and 11¼° for the winter months. Not to dwell on the fact that the term *mean range* is here used in quite another sense than that intended by meteorologists, it is to be lamented that results for *one* year should ever be employed for such uses, as it not unfrequently happens that the mean for one of the three months included is from 4° to 8° higher or lower than the mean for the same month in a series of years. Thus, for July of last year (1861) the mean temperature was about 7° below the average ; and the December mean for 1859 was the lowest on record by about 5°. Instead of 11° for the mean winter temperature, as given in the Colonization Circular, it would probably be nearer the mark to say 13° or 14°. Twenty years ago, as estimated by Judge McCord, the mean winter temperature was given at from 16° to 17°, and the summer mean at 67°—the one differing from the result in the Colonization Circular by 5° or 6°, the other by upwards of 10°.

The year selected for illustration of the climate of Canada must have been otherwise remarkable and exceptional, for we read on the same page that there were 309 fine days, and only 56 on which there was snow or rain in Eastern Canada—results which differ very considerably from those stated in the text.

The tables for Montreal may, without essential variation, be employed to illustrate the climate of the Eastern Townships. Although these as yet possess no established observatory, the following statements may be confidently relied on, as the result of many years' observation.

There are about 150 fine clear days annually, and from 90 to 100 more upon which we should call the weather *fair*. During some years (as in 1862, an exceptional year, in this respect,) it has *rained* on upwards of 100 days; but in general, and including the continuously *rainy, showery,* and *foggy* days, as well as those upon which *snow* falls, the average number scarcely exceeds 100. About 41 inches of water falls in the form of rain, and 11 inches more in that of *snow*, making a total of about 52 inches. The amount of evaporation (allowing 20 inches and 10 inches respectively for summer and winter) is about 30 inches each year. Taking one year with another the direction of the wind is *westerly* for more than five months, but seldom blows from that quarter continuously above three days at a time. Thunder-storms occur from 12 to 15 times a year, and do not last long. Whereas in England not more than from 40 to 50 nights a year are understood to be suited for astronomical observations, this species of work can be prosecuted in the Townships on at least 120 nights.

Occasional severe cold is experienced in the months of December, January, February, and March; but when the temperature is lowest the air is usually clear, as well as conducive to good health and spirits. A moderately low temperature, accompanied with wind, is far less grateful to the feelings than those beautiful bright days for which the climate of Eastern Canada is celebrated, but upon which, judging by the thermometer alone, an European might be led to imagine the weather intolerably cold. Winter may be said to set in generally about the latter part of November, commencing with a *snow-storm* and an easterly wind. The fall of snow is from seven to eight feet for the whole winter, which has usually disappeared from the clearings by the second week in April. It is not uncommon, however, to find the snow later in coming, and the weather not unfit for out-doors farming operations, such as ploughing, &c., up to the close of November. Sometimes the ordinary gardening processes may be begun in the first week of April. As a matter of choice, however, the inhabitants would on the whole welcome the access of snow at any early period after the 15th of November, and its disappearance about the same date in April. In distant parts of Western Canada, where the winter season is a few days later in commencing and where it is said not to linger so long by perhaps 10 or 12 days, the advantage is not near so great as might be supposed, owing to the greater exposure of vegetation to frosts and the impassable character of their spring roads.

The statements of *mean temperature*, whether for summer or winter, do not however furnish adequate means of realizing either the intensity of the cold or the absolute heat occasionally experienced in the Townships. For example, although the *means* for January and February are stated respectively at 13¼° and 17°, yet once or twice during each winter, generally in the night shortly before sunrise, the thermometer sinks as low as 25° or 30° below zero, and even lower sometimes. Again, in the height of summer a temperature of 95° to 100° is occasionally registered, occurring

D

usually in July, and for a short period, at about two or three o'clock P.M. Such incidents of low and high temperature occasion no particular inconvenience, and frequently pass unnoticed except by those who are in the habit of registering meteorological phenomena. Their occasional occurrence is anticipated, and all possible evil consequences provided against in the common modes of building and securing beforehand adequate means of warmth in winter and cool currents of air in summer. In fact, throughout the Eastern Townships, the bodily comfort of the inhabitants generally during the winter season greatly exceeds that of the residents in most houses in England, because fuel is abundant and cheap food plentiful, and the other precautions requisite for protection from cold simple and of easy application. The occasions of intense cold customarily occur early after snow-storms, and are immediately followed by mild weather. A great many persons declare their preference of the winter to the summer season.

From about the latter part of August the weather in the Townships is exceedingly pleasant, and it is doubtful whether, in this respect, the climate of any country in the world is more agreeable.

Towards October the scenery of the country becomes peculiarly attractive, owing to the gradual changes of colour in the foliage which then present themselves. Wherever there are trees in view, the leaves are seen to be *tinted* with various hues of colour. Patches of wood, scattered over the surface, and especially extended masses of forest-trees viewed from any eminence, offer to the eye a very gorgeous spectacle, which, for brightness of colour, variety, and the charming aspect of the whole scene, would inspire disbelief if it were ever so truthfully delineated by the painter's art alone. Some of the most pleasant weather of the whole year often occurs just before the winter sets in, and at that period commonly designated the "*Indian summer.*" This is accompanied with a peculiar hazy appearance skirting the distant horizon. The soft, balmy character of the air then resembles that of the real summer, as if it were, indeed, lingering on and trespassing on the confines of advanced autumn. In the Eastern Townships there is very little of that damp, foggy weather so well known to the inhabitants of London and other parts of England in November, when, as is alleged, the Londoners frequently find it so dark at eight or nine o'clock in the morning that they need artificial light to breakfast by.

As respects salubrity and general suitableness for agricultural purposes, the climate of the Townships is probably superior to that of any other part of Canada. In page 95 of the "Colonization Circular," already referred to, it is stated:—" The climate of Canada East, like that of the Lower Provinces, is unquestionably the most healthy in North America. Disease is unknown among the usual population, except that caused by inequality of diet or imprudent exposure to atmospheric changes. The dryness of the air is shewn by the roofs of houses covered with tin remaining so long bright, and by a charge of gunpowder remaining for weeks uncaked in a gun. . . . If the real excellence of a climate depends upon the earth yielding in perfection and abundance the necessaries of life, or those which constitute the principal articles of food for man and the domestic animals, then Canada East may compare favourably with any part of the world. The steadiness and the uniformity of the summer heat causes all grains and fruits to mature well and with certainty."

In proof that the climate of the Townships is healthful and conducive to longevity, it would be a good test to examine the census returns. Unfortunately, the whole of the census report for 1861 is not yet published. We can, however, in this instance, partially illustrate the matter by means of the returns for the year 1851. In those of the Townships which were included in six counties as then constituted, and which had a population of 94,275, there were returned 2792 persons between 60 and 70 years of age, 1074 between 70 and 80, 327 between 80 and 90, 40 between 90 and 100, with 7 who had survived their hundredth birthday. This statement exhibits a fair proportion to the whole number of people that of the aged. A more extended examination of those returns furnishes similar favourable results as respects the *mortality* at the various periods of life, and especially in the case of children under five years. The people of the Eastern Townships are entirely exempt from *ague*—that terrible scourge which is so prevalent through all the western districts of North American settlement.

It is difficult to approach any discussion of the agricultural capabilities of the Eastern Townships without incurring a risk of seeming to advocate the claims of one section of Canada at the expense of another. This the writer desires by all means to avoid, as being both unpatriotic, and, in its tendency, injurious to the general interests of the country. As in England, France and Belgium, so in Canada, different sections vary in a greater or less degree. Some rich alluvial tracts in all extensive regions are preeminently fitted for the cultivation of the more important cereals—such as wheat—with the attendant disadvantage of being less healthy as the seat of a numerous population. Others surpass in aptitude for the coarser grains and root crops—as oats, barley, potatoes, turnips, and the grasses required for the profitable raising of cattle, sheep, and horses. In a country where labour is dear, as in Canada, it is plain that the agriculturist best consults his interest in applying himself to the cultivation of those articles which yield the greatest profit in proportion to his expenses for work.

Now it happens, that while many of the farmers in the Townships do grow wheat of excellent quality—enough to supply their own wants—they find it more advantageous to attend to the rearing of sheep, cattle, and horses, and the cultivation of grass and the common grains, than to the growing of wheat on an extensive scale. It is, in fact, cheaper for them to allow their section to be supplied with flour from Western Canada than to raise this article themselves in sufficient abundance for the wants of the whole population of Canada East. Thus it happens that Canada East generally is less distinguished than Canada West as a wheat-growing country. But the grass is better, as well as most of the ordinary root crops and coarser grains. The testimony of competent practical judges who have paid great attention to this matter, and whose veracity cannot be impeached, goes to prove that the Eastern Townships are unsurpassed, if equalled, by any other tract in Canada for the purposes of sheep, dairy, and grazing farms.

In the average, the Township farmers raise 40 or 50 bushels of oats per acre, sometimes 80 bushels, or more; from two to three hundred bushels of roots, such as potatoes, &c.; 40 to 60 bushels of maize or Indian corn; and excellent grass year after year from the same fields from one to one and a half tons per acre. The climate and soil are excellently adapted for the cultivation of *hops* and *flax*. Of the last named article, *flax*, it may be confidently stated, that in no part of the world could it be grown of a better quality and to better advantage. The region abounding in pure water—so necessary for the processes by which the fibre is separated from the straw, and on the careful attention to which the quality so mainly depends—with a climate and soil especially adapted for its growth, it is not unlikely that the Eastern Townships may become a great flax-growing country in the course of the next few years, stimulated by the extraordinary and increasing demand for fibre of a fine quality for the Leeds, Dundee, and Belfast markets. The early settlers of the Townships were in the habit of sowing small patches solely as a means of supplying themselves with household linen. The separation of the fibre, and the spinning and weaving, were effected by comparatively rude processes, although a very excellent quality of linen was often produced. The domestic manufacture has, however, decreased much of late years. But the old doctrine that flax-growing impoverishes the soil having been exploded, and replaced by the admission that under a proper system of rotation of crops and attention to ordinary requirements, the land is actually improved in its capabilities for every agricultural purpose, it is believed that advantage will now be taken of the opportunities offered in this direction. Flax is known to be one of the most valuable crops that can be raised, the return per acre being greatly in advance of that for wheat or any other cereal. Recently, a "flax association" has been formed in the Townships, under the auspices of R. W. Henneker, Esq., Commissioner of the British American Land Company, aided by some of the most influential farmers—the main object being to encourage this branch of agriculture by disseminating useful information about the cultivation of flax and its preparation for market.

In the Townships farming is carried on upon every variety of scale—from the clearing of 12 or 15 acres with small loghouse as a homestead up to magnificent farms of several hundreds of acres with substantial dwelling-houses and out-buildings. Uncleared lands can be bought at two or three shillings per acre in some parts and at from 5 up to 25 or 30 dollars per acre for fine large farms, according to extent and situation. The steady persevering cultivator of the soil having a little capital to begin with, can with prudence and tolerable management secure not merely a livelihood but also a comfortable competence, which has indeed, in hundreds of instances, been acquired by persons who had at first no pecuniary funds to start upon.

Owing to causes which the writer does not feel called upon to discuss here, however much it may be a subject of regret, the display of Agricultural products of the Townships at the Great Exhibition is very small indeed. Accordingly, in such objects Mr. Brown of Cowansville, and Mr. Badham of Drummondville, alone received rewards—the former a *Medal* for his *maple sugar*,* and the latter an *Honourable Mention* for sample of *oats*. It appears certain that if the agricultural products and the local manufactures had been adequately represented by specimens prepared in their best fashion, a much larger number of awards would have been assigned to them, and the result altogether such as to present their section of country on a most favourable footing in comparison with any other portion of the British Colonies.

The great natural capabilities of the Eastern Townships as a seat of manufactures has been already alluded to. It is believed that the advantages in this way could scarcely be over-stated. The inhabitants are most desirous that British capitalists should visit the country, look about them, and judge for themselves. In nearly every village and town, as well as in innumerable localities throughout the unsettled parts, there are water privileges to be had on almost any terms that a capitalist could desire. The facilities of a home market will steadily increase, while the low rates of taxation, easy access by railroad to the cities and to the United States and the seaboard, with the contiguity of splendid farming regions, and building materials of all sorts to be had for the labour of procuring them on the spot, invite the attention of all manufacturers who export goods to America under great comparative disadvantages. Machinery driven by water-power can be kept running throughout the year, in winter as well as in summer, as is done in the capital town, Sherbrooke, and throughout the New England States. A theory loosely thrown out some years ago by persons not conversant with these facts, and taken up in a few instances by interested persons—viz., that the water-privileges might prove unavailing in winter, has been entirely exploded. The same thing was alleged formerly respecting the working of Railroads even in England, and during the infancy of those undertakings the suggestion exercised some influence on timid minds. In fact, the grist and saw mills of the Townships are usually kept in operation throughout the winter, unless there should exist some temporary deficiency of water in the smaller streams, or some other cause, rendering it undesirable, in the judgment of their owners, to work them. Local manufactures on a small scale are prosecuted generally by the inhabitants—including various processes in the use of iron and some

* Most of the farmers supply themselves with this article of domestic use from their own *sugaries* or groves of the *maple tree (Acer saccharinum)*. The sap, procured by perforating the trees, is boiled down to the consistence of a syrup that will form into cakes on cooling. Sugar of the finest grain and flavour is thus obtained.

other metals, machine and tool making, various works in wood, carriage making, manufacture of agricultural implements, lime, lumbering, matches, cloths, paper, leather, and so forth. But the manufacturing capabilities are not as yet, in any degree compatible with the ample provisions of nature, turned to account. One instance, however, merits particular mention, one of the local lumbering establishments—that of Messrs. Clarke and Co., at Brompton Falls, a few miles below Sherbrooke—is extensive and well appointed. On these premises are accommodations for the employment of several hundred men and several descriptions of cutting machinery. The out-buildings are numerous, and include various sheds, storehouses, and offices, workshops for repairs, gashouses for supplying their own means of illumination, and stables, besides the day and night boarding-houses for such of the workmen as may not desire to provide their own dwellings. His Royal Highness the Prince of Wales and the Duke of Newcastle inspected these works on the occasion of their late visit to Canada. Messrs. Clarke and Co. export an enormous quantity of timber in the shape of boards, planks, &c., for the United States, and sugar boxes for the West Indies, which reach the seaboard at Portland by the Grand Trunk Railway. They also carry on, during a considerable portion of each year, extensive lumbering operations among the forests contiguous to the head waters of the River St. Francis, many miles above Sherbrooke, aided by the small lakes and affluents of that river.

The inhabitants of those parts of the Townships no doubt experience benefit from the existence of those works, as they furnish employment and assist in creating a home market for agricultural produce.

Increased attention has of late years been paid also to the *mining* capabilities of the Townships, in consequence chiefly of the discovery of great deposits of copper ore.

From *fourteen* different localities, including the Townships of *Upton, Acton, Wickham, Durham, Leeds, Cleveland, Melbourne, Sutton, Chester, Ham, Garthley,* and *Ascot,* very rich specimens of this material are displayed in the Canadian Court at the International Exhibition, of which four or five have been selected by the Jurors as objects of reward. It is believed that a more extended search will prove the presence of similar ores in a great many other localities in the region. When we reflect that it is not very long since the opportunities of producing copper were so small in all North America that the wants of a single sea-port could not be adequately supplied with that metal, we cannot but anticipate that these deposits in the Eastern Townships, so favourably as they are situated for the trade, may soon engage the attention of large capitalists, and contribute materially to the progress and wealth of the country.

There are besides immense quantities of the very best *slate* for roofing and other purposes, and of beautiful *marble, serpentine, chromic iron,* and that very valuable material *steatite* or *soapstone*. Of these materials also fine specimens were sent to the Exhibition, and their exhibitors in some instances were worthily rewarded by medals. An inspection of the

Catalogue for Canada East will shew that in upwards of *forty instances* the mineral products on exhibition were from the Eastern Townships. If the Townships were a poor bleak region, unprovided with water-power, and abundance of timber, limestone, clay, and other building materials, and not blessed with good soil and agricultural facilities, even in that case their very favourable position, with the possession of so much mineral wealth, might be expected to render them a most profitable field for the employment of capital. It must not be understood that the Jurors on minerals based their decisions solely or even principally upon the *quality* of the objects exhibited. They included in their judgments the force and skill which had been employed in the processes of mining and quarrying. Hence those parties in the Townships whose objects on exhibition were not rewarded, or which gained only the second class of awards, have no occasion to feel discouraged at the result; for, as is well known, the mining operations of individuals, or of infant companies embarking on a small scale in undertakings of an exploratory or preliminary character, are not usually so distinguished in those respects as the workmanship of an established and wealthy co-partnery.

CHAPTER V.

INSTITUTIONS OF THE EASTERN TOWNSHIPS — RAILWAYS—EASTERN TOWN-SHIPS' BANK—BRITISH AMERICAN LAND COMPANY—EDUCATION—UNIVERSITY, COLLEGES AND SCHOOLS—THE PRESS—RELIGIOUS, SOCIAL, AND POSTAL MATTERS—AGRICULTURAL SOCIETIES—LOCAL SOCIETIES AND ASSOCIATIONS.

IT is impossible here to offer more than a brief notice of the Institutions of the Eastern Townships. Those which have exercised, or which promise to exercise, the greatest influence upon their general progress, including those which afford the best means of realizing a judgment upon the state of the country and people, will occupy our chief attention.

Railways.—Railway communication has already become familiar by daily experience, for the Township community participate to the full in the advantages afforded by the most gigantic railway line in the world—now called the Grand Trunk Railway of Canada. Its entire course, more than a thousand miles in length, is indicated on the appended map.* From *Sarnia*, on Lake Huron, it passes through several cities of the Upper

* For the use of this map the writer is indebted to the Secretary of the Grand Trunk Railway Company, John M. Grant, Esq., whose ability and most obliging courtesy are known to all who have information to seek or business to transact at their London Office, 21, Old Broad-street.

Province, and reaches the commercial metropolis of Canada, *Montreal*, whence, after crossing the River St. Lawrence by the Victoria Bridge, i diverges towards *Melbourne* and *Richmond* in the heart of the Eastern Townships. At Richmond it divides into two main branches, one leading eastwards to Quebec, and further on to its present termination at Riviere du Loup, below that city and on the south shore of the St. Lawrence ; the other southwards through *Sherbrooke, Lennoxville, Waterville*, and *Coaticooke*, towards *Island Pond* and its ocean terminus at the city of Portland in the United States. Both in the west from *Detroit* beyond Sarnia, and in the east at Portland, as well as at important stations along the line, connections have been perfected with other lines of travel leading to all the principal places on the continent.

The completed Grand Trunk route is marked *red* on the map, and dotted lines shew the course of the proposed Intercolonial Railroad for extending the communication on British territory through New Brunswick and Nova Scotia to the sea at Halifax.

When this great Canadian Railway was projected, and until after some progress had been made in its construction, it was very doubtful whether the territory inhabited by the people of the Eastern Townships would ever be traversed by any portion of the line. Without ignoring the valuable services of others, we may be permitted to say that this result is to be ascribed chiefly to the exertions of a few of the principal residents, whose names will on that account be long held in grateful remembrance by the people. The late Samuel Brooks, and the Hon. A. T. Galt, then Chief Commissioner of the British American Land Company, were most prominent in their influential efforts, and foreseeing, at an early period, the immense importance of the occasion to the lasting interests of their section, were successful in enlisting general support and in securing the route to Portland.

Like all other great public undertakings, the Grand Trunk Railway scheme has, from time to time, been the subject of much controversy, chiefly on account of the vast expense incurred in the construction and putting into operation. With these controversies we have here perhaps no other concern than to express an earnest hope that all who have borne a share of the outlay, and taken a part in the execution of so vast a project, may reap the just reward of their enterprise. Making due allowance for the magnitude and variety of the interests involved—for partizan and sectional feelings on the one hand, and on the other for timidity, interested misrepresentations, and the difficulties necessarily encountered in endeavours to foster extensive traffic in a new country—there is no dispassionate person who would not say that the Grand Trunk Company are entitled to the gratitude of the people of Canada, and to all the support and assistance which can be lawfully given by the Legislature.

So far as the people of Canada are concerned, it may be stated that, notwithstanding its enormous cost, this railroad was a necessary supplement to the other great and expensive public works of the country, the value of which would have been in a great measure sacrificed if the railway scheme had failed of accomplishment.

As respects the Eastern Townships, its construction gave an impulse to progress which has never flagged since. It has conferred on real estate generally an additional value of at least *twenty-five* per cent. Property of various kinds, which could scarcely be parted with at any price, has become saleable. The access afforded both to the leading Canadian markets and to those of the world at large, stimulates activity even in the remote back settlements, and makes the people feel that they are no longer separated by impassable natural obstacles from commercial and social intercourse with the rest of mankind.

Those who knew the Townships twenty years ago will concur in admitting that the Railroad has essentially assisted in advancing them to their present stage of progress. It has given life and breath to many a useful local enterprise, of which, in the absence of the facilities afforded by it, the execution would have been impossible. At this day it is an affair of but a few hours to arrive in the centre of the Townships whether from the seacoast at Portland or from the St. Lawrence at Quebec and Montreal. Letters and newspapers are brought daily, and even twice a day, to all the principal localities—and it is not too much to say, in behalf of the manner in which those services are performed and of the travelling facilities generally, that the people of the Eastern Townships enjoy the benefits of safety, personal comfort, economy, and punctuality, in their railroad communications, in a higher degree than is the case throughout the greater part of England. Strangers visiting England after travelling in Canada are usually surprised by facts of this nature, and especially at finding almost everywhere the want of punctuality and high charges on the express routes which extend to any distance from London.

One particular advantage for which the Eastern Townships are indebted to the organization and proceedings of the Grand Trunk Company merits special mention.

The Company, through the willing and courteous explanations of its officials, published documents, pamphlets, maps, and various other means, has been instrumental in bringing prominently forward into notice the resources and capabilities of this part of Canada. It is not, as some have unreasonably imagined, the interest of the Company to carry the emigrant to the western boundary of Canada on purpose that he may become a settler in the territory of the neighbouring republic. On the contrary, every such passenger, transported beyond the confines of the Province, is, as it were, lost to the Company, while every settler retained in Canada is of some prospective value. Instead of being parted with as a customer of the road, probably for ever, he is likely, as a Canadian, to contribute to its future business in some proportion to his own prosperity. In fact, it must be obvious that the Grand Trunk Company is most deeply interested in promoting the development of resources and the increase of population in all parts of the country through which their line passes.

Through the numerous publications adverted to above, all the more important sections are made known and kept in view, and in this way the Eastern Townships are, as it were, advertised to an extent which under any other circumstances would seem to be impracticable.

There is a second line, connecting the Eastern Townships with Montreal, called the "*Stanstead, Shefford, and Chambly Railway*," completed as far as the village of *Waterloo*, about 30 miles distant from Sherbrooke. On referring to the map of the Townships it will be seen to pass from Montreal towards St. John's on the Richelieu, and thence through the Townships of *Farnham, Granby,* and *Shefford.* Eventually it will be extended through other Townships towards Lake Memphramagog, and further on into the States to connect with the ¡Passumpsic Line of Railway leading to Boston. It is understood that a branch will be constructed so as to join this second line with the Grand Trunk.

The advantages of the Stanstead, Shefford, and Chambly Railway are already sensibly felt by the inhabitants, especially by those who occupy the section west of Sherbrooke. The country through which it passes has already been described as exceedingly fertile and abounding in romantic scenery—and one of the benefits to be expected from this road is the opening up of access to enormous stores of mineral wealth which have hitherto lain dormant. For this valuable addition to the progress of the Eastern Townships the country is indebted chiefly to the forethought and exertions of A. B. Foster, Esq., of Shefford.

The Eastern Townships Bank.—This Institution was chartered by the Provincial Parliament in 1856; its capital stock is 400,000 dollars, in 8000 shares of 50 dollars each. The necessity for its establishment has grown out of the ordinary legitimate business wants of the country, and it is a noticeable fact that it has been put into most successful operation by means of capital raised among the Township people themselves. It pays dividends equal to those of the most prosperous and oldest established banking corporations in the Province. But there is this important difference between those more wealthy establishments and the Eastern Townships Bank, that the latter does not depend for its security upon having a comparatively small number of wealthy stockholders, or upon outside institutions not vitally interested in the welfare of the country forming the scene of operation.

The character of the Bank will be best apprehended from the following passages quoted from a notice appended to its printed By-Laws. "Up to "the date of the organization of the Bank this section of country was "entirely dependent on the City of Montreal and United States Banks "located on the frontier, for all Banking accommodations, and was conse- "quently always liable to be hampered by the necessity those Banks were "under of regulating their action by the frequent fluctuations of business

" in their several localities. . . . . An inspection of the Stock Books
" will shew the wide extent of the Subscriptions scattered over the whole
" of the Eastern Townships and comprising all classes of the community,
" including merchants, mechanics, farmers, professional and business men
" of all kinds. It would perhaps have been easier for the promoters
" to have raised the capital required from a few wealthy individuals, but
" the object in view was both to benefit the country and to provide at the
" same time a safeguard against any speculative action on the part of
" the Bank itself, by creating a wide-spread and deep interest in its well-
" being among the people themselves. When so large a proprietary exists,
" most of them desiring accommodations for carrying on their business, it
" is reasonable to expect that great advances to a few will not be tolerated.
" In fact, the safer business of accommodation in small amounts to the
" many is the rule."

The head-quarters of the Bank are at Sherbrooke, and branches have been established by the directors at *Waterloo, Stanstead,* and *Stanbridge.*

Conformably to the Charter, the whole capital must be paid up by September, 1864. Including those cases in which subscribers have paid their whole subscriptions, the capital paid in, up to April 30th, 1862, amounted to 227,698 dollars, and the accounts shewed 109,546 dollars under the head of *deposits.*

Business was not actually commenced before September, 1859, when the organization was finally completed, and since which period five semi-annual dividends have been paid – the first three at the rate of 6, and the last two at 8, per annum on paid up stock.

Since the breaking out of the civil war in the United States, there has been a partial cessation of several kinds of foreign business hitherto profitable to the Townships, while the Directors of the Bank have felt obliged to avoid all dealings which might cause them loss through the depreciated condition of the American currency. The amounts of the dividends just stated are, therefore, indicative both of the correct principles upon which the proceedings of this institution are regulated and of the prudence and success with which the Directors have carried them out. The President of the Bank is Benjamin Pomroy, Esq., of Compton; and the Directors associated with him are all gentlemen occupying prominent positions in the Townships, and deeply interested themselves in the prosperity of the country.

It should be mentioned here, that the laws of the Province make the most ample provision to guard the country at large from many evils which have been found to infect Banking operations elsewhere. Canadian Chartered Banks are not allowed to commence business before furnishing proof that a certain fixed proportion of the subscribed capital has been actually paid in. Securities are required to be deposited with the Inspector General of the Province, and reports, accompanied by satisfactory vouchers, must be rendered periodically, shewing the precise state of their affairs and published by authority, and their issues of notes or bank bills are prescribed by law in such manner that the amount in circulation shall not exceed certain limits—the general principle followed being to secure the community from inability on the part of the Banks to redeem their obligations on demand. Depositors and other creditors of a Bank are further secured by a provision of the law making the stockholders responsible in their private capacities in the event of the assets of the corporation being deemed insufficient to liquidate its liabilities. The responsibility referred to is, for each stockholder, the amount of the shares held by him; or, sometimes, as is the case with the Eastern Townships Bank, it extends to double that amount. Moreover, special clauses in the Charter prescribe limits to the amount of indebtedness that may lawfully be incurred, with penalty for excess, requiring also that statements of affairs be made monthly and published. No person can be a Director without being a British subject, seven years a resident in Canada, and the owner of at least twenty shares of the stock. To prevent possible embezzlement of the funds of the bank by officials, that offence is adjudged to be *felony*, punishable, under the Act, by imprisonment extending, according to circumstances, from two years in any jail to seven years in the penitentiary.

The Chartered Banks of Canada have thus been placed on so secure a footing, and their general management has been characterized by so much prudence and success, that the whole system has been pronounced admirable by all competent judges who have taken the trouble to acquaint themselves with the matter.

In the case of the Eastern Townships Bank, which is also the Government Bank of Deposit for all public offices south of the St. Lawrence—failure appears to be well nigh impossible as regards all the legitimate purposes of banking.

The writer has been the more desirous to state the particulars of this local institution, because it not unfrequently happens that persons emigrating from the British Isles to the Townships, or sending remittances, in ignorance of its existence, place their funds so that they can be drawn only through some distant banking house, located, perhaps, in Toronto, or some other town in Upper Canada. This is not only altogether unnecessary, but is attended with expense, delay, and other inconvenience.* It should also be mentioned that, whether in the form of shares in the capital stock, or of deposit on interest, money, which is invested at the customary

---

* Persons having occasion to remit money from Great Britain, to be received in the Eastern Townships, should cause it to be paid in to the bank of Messrs. Glyn, Mills and Co. Lombard Street, London, with the direction that it is to pass to " The Eastern Townships Bank, Sherbrooke, Canada East," in which case it is remitted by the earliest mail through the " City Bank of Montreal," the city correspondent of the Eastern Townships Bank, at whose office in Sherbrooke the amount would be paid to the parties entitled to receive it. In the case of purchasing shares in the Bank stock, the process would be similar, accompanied with the requisite instructions to the cashier.

low rates in the Old Country, for the benefit of residents in the Townships, can now be as securely lodged there, on the spot, and becomes productive of much greater revenue to the recipients. With a Bank of their own under the vigilant control of the resident stockholders, and the management of responsible Directors nominated by themselves, it would be difficult to overrate the advantage of this very useful institution, whether we consider its subserviency to the general interests of the section, or its convenience in the above named particulars to those who have occasionally to transact money business with correspondents in distant countries.

Up to a recent period, and during the earlier history of the Townships, banking facilities were afforded by an *Agency*, or Branch Bank, maintained in Sherbrooke by the City Bank of Montreal. It is believed that this establishment, so far as it could safely spare any portion of its moderate capital from requirements in the city, accorded all reasonable accommodation to the pecuniary wants of the community in and around Sherbrooke. Its connection with the Townships has not altogether ceased, since the Agency is still kept open for most kinds of money business, while its head office in Montreal acts as the city correspondent of the Eastern Townships Bank.

The British American Land Company.—The interests of the Eastern Townships have now for thirty years been so intimately associated with the proceedings of this Company and their employés in Canada, that no account of the condition and progress of this section of country could be made intelligible without setting forth in some detail the nature of their operations. In this connection the writer feels called upon to premise that he is entirely unbiassed by those partizan political feelings which in Canada are so frequently permitted to affect a judgment upon the actions of incorporated bodies. It is well known that sentiments unfavourable to corporations are often loosely expressed by people who take no trouble to think for themselves, and who, unacquainted with the real facts, accept, as such, the exaggerations and partial statements that sometimes find a hearing even in the Provincial Parliament. However much such a state of things is to be regretted—the necessary incidental accompaniment possibly, of the pioneering days of a youthful people endeavouring to work out for themselves the destinies of self-government—there does exist a certain amount of *touchiness* on those subjects, which, whenever it is worked upon, has the harmful effect of strengthening prejudices, and of preventing those who may be under its influence from judging fairly about matters in which their own interests are concerned.

Fortunately for the Townships, however, prejudices of that nature have not been able to prevent them from deriving very great advantages from their connection with the British American Land Company, although this body has not been exempt from occasional attacks growing out of and founded upon those feelings.

The Company, in England, is represented by a Court of Directors, consisting of a Governor, Deputy Governor, and ten other gentlemen, who, with duly appointed auditors, a Solicitor, and a Secretary, hold their business meetings in London.* In Canada, their affairs are conducted by a *Commissioner*, whose head-quarters are established in the town of Sherbrooke, and who presides over the duties of a numerous staff of officers and agents required in the management of the local business.

In the selection of their Commissioners the Company have been singularly fortunate, and indirectly instrumental in benefiting the province at large. Some years ago the office was filled by *Mr. Galt*. In his case, the Township people themselves subsequently endorsed the choice by electing him to represent Sherbrooke in Parliament, a position which he has continued, in virtue of successive elections, to hold to this day; and, it may be added, the whole of Canada has in some sense expressed a concurrence and appreciation of the value of his services by his advancement to the post of Finance Minister in the Government. The successor of Mr. Galt, and the present Commissioner of the Company, is Mr. Henneker, who took up his residence in Sherbrooke some years ago. The active countenance which this gentleman has given to all measures for promoting progress, his business tact—so valuable in local matters—the fairness which characterizes his dealings with the people who have transactions with the Company, as well as his kindly intercourse with all, and his high social qualifications, have rendered him an object of universal esteem in the Townships. A Company which has virtually *given* to the service of the colony two such men would be, on that account alone, entitled to grateful consideration.

In the great work of colonizing and settling the territory of the Townships, the Company have necessarily exercised a very strong influence in consequence of being so large a proprietor, and because this description of proprietary is unaccompanied by the disadvantages of absenteeism. For the wild lands held, and for their property generally, it pays the legal taxes, and bears its share in the construction of the roads, bridges, &c., requisite to the opening up of new settlements. The lands possessed are not all in one block, but distributed through various distinct townships, in which every sale that occurs under its auspices, and every improvement effected, confer additional value upon adjacent properties. Immense opportunities of water-power are owned by the Company at Sherbrooke, and lower down the St. Francis on the opposite bank to Clarke's Mills, and in a great many other localities. In the application of this, more particularly at Sherbrooke, mills and other works have been erected at the Company's expense. These are placed by lease at the disposal of manufacturers and persons willing to carry them on upon equitable terms. In many instances all the capital

* Offices, 35½, New Broad Street.

required for starting has been furnished by the Company, who, through their Commissioner and agents, assist in every way that can be reasonably expected, both as regards the prosecution of manufactures, maintenance in a state of repair and in rebuilding, and in rendering as small as possible losses which occur through fire and unavoidable accident. The Company have, in fact, virtually founded the town of Sherbrooke, the principal sources of its increase in wealth and population being the natural results of their own business or consequences of proceedings for developing the general resources of the section in which they have always taken a conspicuous part. In contributing to bring the railroad through that part of Canada, in promoting the establishment of the Eastern Townships Bank, and in various smaller undertakings of local importance, the Company has done that at the proper time and in the proper manner, which, if then omitted, would have left the Townships in a very much more backward condition than they have now reached.

In the sale of their lands, "the terms vary according to circumstances —the principal object being to secure an industrious and thrifty class of Settlers.

"A small payment at the time of sale is usually demanded to insure that the application is made in good faith; and time is given for the payment of the balance of the purchase-money.

"The price of Land varies from Ten Shillings to Twenty Shillings per acre, but the average price of good Farming Land is about Twelve Shillings and Sixpence per acre.

"Improved Farms, with Buildings complete, may be purchased in any part of the Eastern Townships, at from £200 to £750 for a lot of 200 acres.

"Town Lots, in Sherbrooke Town, for trade or manufacturing purposes, may be obtained at from £30 to £50 per quarter-acre building lots, or rented, with water-power for manufacturing purposes."

The terms of the Company for water-power are very much more favourable to the lessee than those customarily afforded throughout Massachusetts and in New England.

The foregoing statement about the British American Land Company, as a Township Institution, would be essentially defective if the writer neglected to refer to its co-operation, through its officials, in all efforts for advancing the educational, social, and religious welfare of the inhabitants. The Commissioner is a trustee of the local university, and exercises a most useful influence upon its counsels. Assistance in money and donations of land have been contributed by the Company in order to promote religious worship in the settlements. The officers of the Company and their families add in a considerable degree, by their mere presence, to the social attractions of the neighbourhood, rendering it an object to new settlers having families to locate themselves within reach of intercourse with them. They are all gentlemen of intellectual character, and much respected in the community. The important office of Mayor of Sherbrooke is now filled by J. G. Robertson, Esq., who presented the Address on behalf of the Town on the occasion of the Prince of Wales' visit, and was formerly for many years one of the principal officers of the British American Land Company.

We shall now turn our attention to those institutions which are more expressly intended to promote intellectual, moral, and social progress. Without these, it is scarcely necessary to say, no country, however bountifully endowed with natural resources, can be held to be in the possession of the essential requirements to happiness needed most by those who, leaving behind them the civilization of Great Britain, go to establish homes in the colonies.

Education.—In order to form an idea of the state and prospects of education in the Eastern Townships, it is necessary, in the first place, to say a few words about the laws of the Province framed in that behalf.

The State places opportunities of education within the reach of every child. Whether the opportunities be made use of or not, taxes are required to be paid for educational purposes by all parents and owners of property. The public schools, more particularly the subject of Legislative enactment, are classified in three grades,—*Primary*, or *Common Schools; Model Schools;* and *Academies*, or *Grammar Schools*—in which the instruction given rises by gradation from the most elementary up to the higher branches, for the further prosecution of which recourse must be had to colleges and universities, which latter grades in Eastern Canada, are included under the name of *Superior Schools*. The municipalities are divided into two or more *School Districts*, in each of which school-buildings must be erected and maintained, and in each municipality five *School Commissioners* are elected to form a corporation, to hold office for three years, and to execute various duties imposed on them by law. The duties include all objects appertaining to the management and disposal of property applicable in their districts to public education, the appointment and removal of schoolmasters and schoolmistresses, the regulation of course of study and fees, the raising of money from assessment and other sources, with power to prosecute persons who may neglect to pay their lawful portion of school rates.

In conjunction with the foregoing provisions, *Boards of Examiners* are established, whose members are nominated by the Governor General with a jurisdiction extending, in the case of each Board, over the school districts contained in several counties, for the purpose of certifying the qualifications of teachers, who must hold diplomas from these Boards before appointment

to office by the School Commissioners. The regulations under which the Board of Examiners act, are prescribed by the *Council of Public Instruction*, whose provisions in that behalf, and ¹n regard to the text books to be used in the schools, become law, after receiving the approval of His Excellency the Governor General.

Every candidate for the office of teacher must be provided with certificates of age and of good moral character—the latter to be signed by the minister of his or her own faith, and by school commissioners of the district lived in during the previous six months.

For the due execution of the various provisions of the Educational Laws, there is a *Superintendent of Education*, appointed by the Governor General. The superintendent, who has a seat in the Council of Public Instruction, receives the reports required periodically from school commissioners and boards of examiners, and prepares annually a statement exhibiting the condition and progress of education throughout the country. He also receives and distributes, under the sanction of the Governor, the public funds allotted for educational purposes.

It would require a large volume to present in detail an account of the scheme of education as established by law for the benefit of the present and future inhabitants of Canada East. In this section of the Province very great progress has been made in all essential particulars. Under the auspices of the present Superintendent of Education for Canada East, the Hon. P. O. Chauveau, who has now been in office a number of years sufficient to test the applicability of the laws to the wants of the people, the advancement has been, proportionally to circumstances, considerably more rapid than in the western section of the Province. It is due to that gentleman to say, that those who have watched the course of things during his administration, including persons of a different religious creed from his own, are agreed in ascribing to his tact, enlightened views, and other admirable qualifications for office, the largest share of credit for success attained. Indeed, many of those who were at first quite opposed to the introduction of existing modifications and amendments upon the older educational laws, have quite changed in their sentiments on witnessing the ability and impartiality with which the duties of his important office have been discharged.

It is perhaps well to mention that the educational scheme embraces the maintenance of three *Normal schools* for instructing and training teachers who are made to prosecute a course having special reference to the duties of their profession.

In about fifty of the Eastern Townships, those most settled and occupied by English speaking and Protestant inhabitants, the latest published statements of the Superintendent report upwards of 500 Educational

E

Institutions of all kinds, attended by about 20,000 pupils. Amongst these are included 1 *university* and 2 *colleges*, attended by upwards of 800, together with 22 *academies* having more than 2000 pupils, and, of *primary and model schools* about 490, with about 15,000 scholars. The academies and other schools of the Townships are included in two large districts, in each of which an *Inspector*, acting under the authority of the Superintendent, is constantly employed. The duties of the inspectors are very onerous, requiring for their discharge the services of gentlemen of a very high order of ability. In their intercourse with the School Commissioners and Board of Examiners and for visiting the various schools under their local supervision, they must possess a combination of qualifications very difficult of acquisition, comprising a perfect knowledge of details of the Educational Laws, familiarity with the habits of the people, and experience in the arts of teaching and training youth so as to enable them to furnish useful suggestions to the teachers as well as to take up readily any branch of instruction for the purposes of examination on the occasion of their official visits. The post of Inspector in the important district which includes Sherbrooke and Townships in its vicinity has been filled for some years past with remarkable ability by Mr. Henry Hubbard. The Inspectors render periodical reports to the Superintendent, who is himself legally empowered to inspect affairs and demand direct reports from any of the boards, officials, and institutions mentioned above.

Under such arrangements, together with others, which it would be tedious to detail, a provision is made for executing the requirements of the law in regard to Public Education in the Townships. The whole business is, in fact, placed on a footing that would be pronounced highly satisfactory in comparison with the state of things existing in most European communities.

Although the amounts to be raised by assessment in the Municipalities need not necessarily be more than equal to those allotted for educational purposes from the public funds, yet they are not unfrequently and voluntarily doubled. The ratio of attendance is about one in six of an age fit for school, which exceeds that given by the returns of most countries. At the same time attendance is not absolutely compulsory, for this would be repugnant to the disposition of the people, but certainly it is encouraged by the requirement that every man must pay school rates whether he has children at school or not.

The public schools adverted to derive additional support from tuition-fees, payable by the attendant pupils, who are, however, in cases of indigence, excused from any such charge. The fees chargeable in the primary schools may not exceed *two shillings*, and at the discretion of the

School Commissioners may be reduced to *threepence* per month. The Commissioners are not empowered to establish a higher rate than £150 for the building of a model school or academy, and £75 is the legal limit for a primary school. The lower grades of schools are not required to be kept in operation more than 8 months in each year, thus affording time for scholars of an age to work to assist in agricultural and other labours.

In some of the public schools, especially in some of the *academies*, the opportunities, both as to mode of teaching and appliances, and as regards extent of knowledge to be gained, are very superior. For the most part, however, they are limited to the more common, useful, and elementary branches of instruction, the provisions of the law contemplating chiefly what is necessary or indispensable in the way of general education. The terms *College* and *Classical Colleges*, as respects Lower Canada, are usually applied to those institutions which, on a higher footing than the *academies*, include some additional and special provision for teaching the elements of classical learning and of science. They receive a larger portion of public money towards their expenses than the other schools. In the classification adopted by the Superintendent, the classical colleges are placed in order after *universities*, and having what are styled *industrial colleges* intervening between them and the academies, which latter are placed fourth on the list.

In the Eastern Townships there is one industrial college with upwards of 60 pupils and situated at Sherbrooke.

Of the grade of Classical Colleges, there is also one, established at Richmond, and incorporated a few years ago under the name of *St. Francis College*. This institution is attended by upwards of 100 pupils, and has been affiliated to the McGill College of Montreal. It receives about 1100 dollars a year in aid from the public funds, and is supported by the efforts of private individuals, who are for the most part resident in the vicinity of Richmond and Melbourne. The building, which is of brick, is situated on an eminence near the line of railway.

The most important of the Educational Institutions located in the Eastern Townships is the University at Lennoxville. It was incorporated in the year 1843, under the name of "Bishop's College," in consideration of the active part taken and the munificent contributions to its endowment made by its chief founder, the present Bishop of Quebec. Foreseeing that the time would arrive when the youth of the country would need access to opportunities of prosecuting studies in the highest branches of literature and science, and anxious to secure in the future university a Faculty of Divinity for the education of candidates for the ministry in the Established Church, his Lordship, with the advice and assistance of many friends resident in the cities and in the vicinity of the site selected, entered upon the arduous task of founding an institution of that highest class in the Eastern Townships. It went into operation in 1845, at first with a very slender staff, and encountering, as a matter of course, various obstacles incidental to the circumstances of a new country. In due season, however, and in addition to the provincial charter of incorporation, it received the Royal charter conferring upon it the privileges of an university. It has now been in operation about 17 years. Its buildings consist of a plain brick structure, laid out internally in lecture rooms and accommodations for resident students, communicating in one direction with a handsomely-built wing appropriated as a residence for the chief officer. At the other end the main building is connected with a large Dining Hall, over which apartments are fitted up for the use of the divinity students, having beyond it the College Chapel, a handsome edifice of brick and stone, which, though on a smaller scale than is customary in the European colleges, is probably superior in simple beauty and internal equipments to anything of the same kind yet erected in America. It is roofed with slate, procured from Walton's quarry in the Townships, and the interior woodwork, including the panelling, stalls, &c., is made of the *Butternut* tree (*Juglans Cathartica*), grown in the neighbouring forests. Within the past two years extensive additions have been made, at a cost of from 25,000 to 30,000 dollars, laid out principally in the construction of a very fine building, also of brick and stone, for the use of the Junior Branch and Grammar School of the College, which had previously occupied quarters in the village at some distance from the new structure. A little beyond this last stands the residence of the Rector in charge of the Junior Department. These new buildings are far in advance of any others in the Townships, and the lofty hall appropriated to the use of the Grammar School is superior in dimensions and equipments to anything of the kind that can be found in Lower Canada. The site of the university is on a slope contiguous to the confluence of the two rivers whose banks are occupied by the village of Lennoxville, and its buildings present to the eye a very pleasing appearance from almost every point of view, surrounded as they are by scenery of the most picturesque and charming description.

As some particulars relative to this institution are mentioned by the writer whose letters are appended to this summary, it is unnecessary here to enter into them at any great length. It receives aid from the public funds to the extent of about 2000 dollars a year. The number of its pupils, including those both of the higher and of the lower branches or departments, have amounted to about 180 during the past few terms. In its aims it embraces all the legitimate objects of scholastic, collegiate, and

niversit;
ssociate
Montreal
of religi
by the r
sessing a
lengthen
fundame
modern
lege in
of Med
and als
an app
belong
of whi
the on
especi
that y
instit
T
Vice-
with
Depa
instr
in the
vision
the co
In

university education, and, without being in any sense exclusive, it does not dissociate, as is the case with its Protestant rival, the McGill College of Montreal, the work of education from special recognition of the obligations of religion—one daily attendance in the College Chapel being required by the regulations. It differs also from the institution just named in possessing a Divinity Chair, as well as in devoting a more strict and more lengthened attention to the classics and to pure mathematics, as the two fundamental branches of collegiate learning. The customary branches of modern and general science are included in its course. The McGill College in Montreal, having attached itself to the previously existing faculties of Medicine and Law, for each of which the city had long been famous, and also to the old-established High School, is able, on occasions, to suggest an appearance of force and progress, which, strictly speaking, do not belong to any of the three Universities of Lower Canada, and in the face of which inferences have sometimes been drawn to the disparagement of the one founded in the Townships. But the truth is the country itself, and especially the Protestant portion of the community, have not yet made that progress in numbers and wealth necessary to the full development of institutions of the highest class.

The present staff of the University at Lennoxville consists of a Principal, Vice-Principal, Bursar, Librarian, and four Professors in the Arts' Faculty, with one in that of Divinity. One of the Professors is Rector of the Junior Department and Grammar School, and has under him a sufficient staff of instructors ranking as College Tutors. Each Professor occupying a chair in the University is required by the regulations to exercise a certain supervision over the work done in the Junior Branch and School in relation to the course of instruction in his own special department.

In a country where the French language is necessarily so much used it became important to provide definitely for that subject. Accordingly, a professor of the French language and literature was recently appointed. In due season, when the growth of the neighbouring town of Sherbrooke affords the requisite facilities, and when the progress and wants of the country render it necessary, it is contemplated to establish in the university the faculties of *Law* and *Medicine*.

In the junior department and school, which are attended by youths from various places in Upper and Lower Canada and from the Lower Provinces, much encouragement is given to healthful out-doors exercises, and to physical training, the regular services of the drill-sergeant being employed in that behalf.

Had this institution been founded in either of the principal cities of Eastern Canada, instead of being located in the Townships, it would doubtless have earlier attained to its present stage, and avoided some of the numerous obstacles it has met with. At one time, indeed, through unforeseen deficiencies in its then slender revenue, the work must have been suspended, if not finally closed, but for the timely assistance and liberality of its friends in Quebec.

Since then its progress has derived a strong impulse from the countenance of the Metropolitan of Canada, who has taken a lively interest in all its concerns. The annual convocations of the university are presided over by the Chancellor, the Hon. Mr. Justice McCord, who also, as well as other influential gentlemen of the city of Montreal, have contributed most materially to its advancement. The last annual meeting, held in June of the present year, was attended by Sir F. Williams, Commander of the Forces in Canada, and by numerous other distinguished visitors, and, judging from the interest shewn on this and the like occasions during the past few years, there is reason to anticipate its attaining ultimately to that measure of usefulness and strength which shall serve to perpetuate its existence.

But it must be admitted that there is much remaining to be accomplished. Its library, and museum, and endowment fund are still very incomplete, and the heavy expenses entailed by the erection of the new buildings have placed the university in a position to need pecuniary aid.

The Prince of Wales, when His Royal Highness visited Canada, gave the college £200, which sum was appropriated in founding a prize, to be bestowed in his name annually for scholarship and merit. The people in many parts of the Eastern Townships, as well as benefactors resident in Quebec, Montreal, and elsewhere, have subscribed, in proportion to their means, towards relieving the institution from the pressure of its building expenses, and it is hoped others may be found to assist in removing it altogether. It would be difficult to over-estimate the influence for good which a well-appointed Protestant University is calculated to exercise hereafter in that part of Her Majesty's dominions, in the interest of learning and good morals, in fostering loyalty, and in strengthening the bulwarks of civil and religious liberty.

Before finally leaving the subject of education in the Townships, it may be proper to allude to the *Educational Journal*, published monthly both in French and English, under the auspices of the department presided over by the Superintendent of Education in Eastern Canada, the Hon. P. O. Chauveau. It is a work of very great merit and usefulness, and, no doubt, was chiefly instrumental in influencing the Judges on Educational Appliances at the International Exhibition to award a Medal to that gentleman. Although not peculiar to the Townships—indeed, it is printed in Montreal

—this journal is largely distributed there, and falls into the hands of many of the teachers and others concerned in the progress of education. It abounds with information on topics of interest to persons of that class, keeping them acquainted with every occurrence of note affecting them or appertaining to their pursuits. Official notices are published in it, discussions on the teaching of various branches, original poetry, narratives, copies of reports, summaries, and valuable extracts from other publications. The general tone and style are excellent, tending to inspire loyal and patriotic feelings. There can be no doubt but that it serves a very useful purpose in co-operation with other means of sustaining and promoting educational interests throughout the Townships. The work, moreover, is supplied to persons concerned in education at the low rate of four shillings sterling for a year's subscription, for both English and French copies, or for either, each monthly number containing about 20 large pages of two columns, and very well got up as to type and paper.

We shall conclude this part of our summary with mentioning the *Teachers' Associations*, consisting of teachers of all classes, and persons, officially or otherwise, connected with educational pursuits in the Townships. Their meetings are held at intervals of six months in different towns or villages, and are usually well attended, and continued during two or three successive days. The discussions which take place, interspersed with the delivery of written addresses and of speeches, are of a most instructive and interesting character. The meetings are open to the public, and a general holiday is kept up by the inhabitants of the neighbourhood, and hospitalities of all kinds indiscriminately extended to visitors. It is easy to see that such proceedings are calculated to produce much advantage in furtherance of educational objects generally.

For the establishing of the Teachers' Association, and for its operation in attracting public attention usefully to a great cause, the Townships are indebted chiefly to the services of the Rev. C. Pearl of Waterville, and J. H. Graham, Esq., of St. Francis College, the active zeal and eloquence of these gentlemen being most conspicuous at every session.

The Press.—Within the memory of persons still living there were only about five newspapers published in all Canada, and almost confined in their circulation to the cities of Quebec and Montreal. At the present time there are six newspapers issued in the Townships alone, exclusive of another published at St. Johns, and which ought perhaps to be counted as virtually belonging to the local press. In the year 1837 or 1838 a paper was started in the then inconsiderable village of Sherbrooke, entitled the "*Sherbrooke Gazette and Eastern Townships Advertiser.*" The ability with which this publication has been conducted has been already adverted to, and it is still sustained the first in rank amongst its more youthful competitors by the largest circulation.

The following remarks, extracted from Lovell's Canada Directory, published in 1858, page 1145, and there made use of in reference to the journalism of the Province at large, possess a special applicability to the circumstances of the Eastern Townships:—" The information itself should " prove alike suggestive and instructive. It encourages the belief that the " moral and intellectual advancement has kept pace with its political and " material progress, and it inculcates very earnestly upon all the duty and " necessity of adopting such measures as may best preserve the character " and usefulness of the periodical press. . . . . . . In variety of " information and in moral sentiment the newspaper literature of Canada " will compare favourably with that of any other land; while, through the " unexampled liberality and cordial co-operation of the Legislature, carried " into effect by the untiring exertions of the Post-office Department, it has " been able to find free access to the homes of our people, and has thus " brought to the door of the most humble a blessing which has been regarded " as belonging exclusively to the luxuries of the Old World."

There is only one newspaper in the Eastern Townships which is issued oftener than once weekly. This is the " *Leader*," published also in the town of Sherbrooke every Tuesday and Friday.

The other Township papers are " *The Stanstead Journal*," commenced a few years later than the *Sherbrooke Gazette;* the " *Shefford County Advertiser*," of Granby; the " *Advertiser*," printed in the village of Waterloo; and the " *Richmond Guardian*," published at Richmond every Friday.

The facilities furnished by the Post-office and railways enable most people to receive their papers on the day of their issue, which is also the case with such city newspapers as find a circulation in the Townships.

In the *Reading Room* of the local university most of the leading provincial periodicals are also received, as well as several of the principal British newspapers. The ordinary annual cost of subscription to the Eastern Township papers is six shillings sterling.

Religion.—The intercourse of the members of the different religious denominations scattered through the Eastern Townships is characterised by mutual Christian kindness and forbearance to a degree which is not generally experienced in other countries. Persons of all religious creeds are on terms of perfect equality, politically, and in the eye of the law, none either possessing or attempting to exercise exclusive privileges, or comporting themselves in a manner calculated to give offence to the feelings of others.

Of the Protestant population, those belonging to the United Church of England and Ireland are relatively the most numerous. They have churches in all the older and more settled localities, and about 35 pastors occupying fields of labour in the Townships, which are included within the limits of the two Diocesan districts of Quebec and Montreal.

The other Protestant denominations, of whom the most numerous are the Presbyterians, Wesleyan and other Methodists, and Congregationalists, have also their places of worship and ministers stationed in all the principal centres. In the town of Sherbrooke there is a large church, built some years ago by the Roman Catholics, and contiguous to it a seminary for the use of members of that creed resident in the town or within a moderate distance.

It is a happy circumstance, in view of the welfare and progress of the Townships, that the harmonious feelings above referred to should be so generally prevalent; nor is there any just reason for believing that the instincts and good sense of the majority of the more enlightened inhabitants will not always in future suffice to repress the growth of less favourable sentiments.

Other Local Institutions.—We must now allude briefly to some other features indicative of the condition of the Townships.

The agricultural interests of the Eastern Townships are protected and fostered by means of *Agricultural Societies,* formed in the several counties, receiving, in addition to the subscriptions of their members, aid from the Provincial funds. Their operations, which include the periodical holding of *Shows* of animals and of all kinds of farm produce, with the distribution of prizes, are conducted under the auspices of a special branch of the Government. It should be mentioned also that a Provincial Show is held annually in one or other of the principal places of Canada East for the exhibition of everything relating to agricultural industry.

The Provincial Show is sometimes held in Sherbrooke. It took place there in 1855, and was opened by the Governor-General, Sir Francis B. Head, attended by a number of distinguished persons from various parts of the Province. During the present year (in September, 1862), it is appointed to be again held in the capital of the Eastern Townships. As these gatherings afford opportunities of free personal intercourse among the farmers, and for competition in every department of agriculture, they serve at once to manifest its condition and progress, and to stimulate observation and further efforts in behalf of this great fundamental basis of all wealth.

An impulse has been given recently to the agricultural opportunities by the establishment of a *Fair,* held at Sherbrooke on the first Wednesday in every month. For this great improvement the Townships are indebted to the enlightened exertions of the Commissioner and other officials of the British and American Land Company, who saw that the existing facilities were incommensurate with the wants of the country. The Fair is chiefly for the sale of cattle, horses, sheep, hogs, &c. The grounds on which it is held adjoin the railway station in the town, having every convenience for loading and unloading without risk, and including a weighing house and complete arrangements for the transaction of business. The undertaking proved highly successful last season, under the personal supervision of Mr. Kellam, a well-known agriculturist of Compton. At present its immediate arrangements are placed under the charge of Mr. Pennayer, of Sherbrooke, who has long been connected with the Land Company, and is intimately conversant with the agricultural concerns of the Townships.

The Fairs are well attended, and by attracting dealers from Montreal and Quebec, and by bringing face to face the farmers of the Townships, and purchasers from all parts, benefit the interests of both parties, to the exclusion of middle-men and intermediate agents, by whom such business used formerly to be executed throughout the country.

The formation of a local association for promoting the cultivation of flax as a staple production of the Townships, has already been alluded to.

As the country is so essentially dependent upon the state and progress of agriculture, everything relating to it assumes an importance that could hardly be over-rated. The local newspapers, therefore, are usually found to contain judicious extracts from the agricultural and horticultural publications of other countries, besides which the *Agricultural Journal*, issued in the Province under the auspices of a Department of the State, as well as similar periodicals published in the United States, keep people informed of all the improvements of the day.

Under all the circumstances which have been alluded to, it is scarcely possible that the Eastern Townships should not make progress in all branches of agricultural industry.

In connection with local facilities appertaining to the general advantage of the community, it is proper to allude to such as grow out of the provisions of the laws for

" Promoting the development of mechanical talent among the people of
" the Province, by disseminating instruction in mechanics and kindred
" sciences, extending encouragement to arts and manufactures, and
" stimulating the ingenuity of mechanics and artizans by means of dis-
" tinctions awarded on the same principle as has been already so success-
" fully applied to the encouragement of agriculture."

Under these laws, a " Board of Arts and Manufactures for Lower Canada," has been created. The enactments contemplate a connection between and joint co-operation of a Central Board in Montreal, and the Mechanics' Institutes of the country parts. Such institutions, under the designation of "Mechanics' Institutes, and Library Associations," do indeed exist in towns and villages of the Eastern Townships, although they may not, as yet, have produced all the advantages usually expected from them. Their meetings are sometimes well attended, affording opportunities of self-improvement, and, during the winter season more especially, of spending evenings profitably, through the services of professional persons and other residents.

Of several other local associations, for the promotion of religious objects, temperance societies, and so forth, it is not considered necessary here to offer any description, as it might prove tedious, as well as superfluous, to discuss matters so well known, and proceedings so similar in their nature everywhere.

CONCLUSION.

WE shall close this summary account with a few additional particulars of information relating to houses, farms, settling upon cleared and uncleared lands, and in the villages, embodying in these some brief reference to the classes of persons whose removal to the Eastern Townships might be attended with happy results both to themselves and the country.

The houses of the people are, for the most part, built of wood. In the capital town, as well as in some of the larger villages, there are buildings of brick or stone. The wooden buildings are so constructed as to continue comfortable and otherwise serviceable, without any great cost for repairs, for a period of twenty-five to forty years, or more. The cost is, compared with houses of corresponding pretensions in England, very small, so that the farmers, and nearly all the business people and private residents, build or purchase their own habitations. A dwelling, which in England would cost from five to seven hundred pounds sterling, is customarily finished at about half that expense, notwithstanding the higher prices paid in Canada for the unskilled labour which may be needed in the work. It is a great advantage that alterations and additions to existing buildings may be inexpensively made, owing to the nature of the materials required, and the facility with which they can be everywhere procured. Good taste is often displayed, especially in the vicinity of the towns and villages, in the appearance of smaller dwelling houses, such as suffice for moderately large families, and have not cost for their construction more than £125 to £175 sterling. A family can usually buy a good-sized and neatly finished house in a village, recently built, with outbuildings, fences, &c., complete, and an acre or more of land attached, for about £200 to £350; or where none are vacant or for sale, the same may be procured through the services of resident artizans and contractors.

Land suitable for building purposes is procurable in the villages at about £20 to £100 for an acre, according to situation and other circumstances. In many cases the cost of the ground is not one half of the sum named. Artizans and persons desirous of establishing themselves in business near water privileges, can usually purchase the necessary ground, and erect their buildings at inconsiderable rates. Such persons coming into the Townships, with only a little capital to commence upon, are welcome everywhere, and can do much for themselves to spare the outlay of money necessarily attendant upon hiring the labour and services of others. In some parts, indeed, where thriving settlements have been commenced, suitable lots can be had at the most insignificant prices, in consequence of the desire of enterprising owners of land, and of the settlers already established, to promote the growth of the neighbourhood. Whenever land, building lots, water privileges, mill-works, or dwellings, are sold to a purchaser, easy terms of payment are accorded, rendering it next to certain that a man having small capital, and starting in his business at once, will soon be enabled to possess the freehold. Of course there must be temperance, and the exercise of ordinary common sense in the management of one's affairs, as, without these essential qualities, a person cannot fairly expect to succeed in life in any part of the world.

The farm buildings, from the small *log* dwellings and out-houses in the back settlements, up to the comfortable neat-looking structures, equal to those of the villages, and occupied by substantial farmers, are constructed at rates of expenditure too various to admit of description here. A farmer can usually provide his buildings, deriving materials from his own grounds, and contributing the assistance of himself and his own labourers, or with the reciprocated assistance of his neighbours, at an outlay in money not exceeding one-half of the sums mentioned for village habitations. This is a very common mode of proceeding, especially when a new dwelling-house is to be erected on the same farm, and when repairs are to be made or new out-buildings constructed. But those who buy farms partially or wholly cleared commonly find the requisite buildings already prepared. The prices of such farms as have been last mentioned vary of course according to

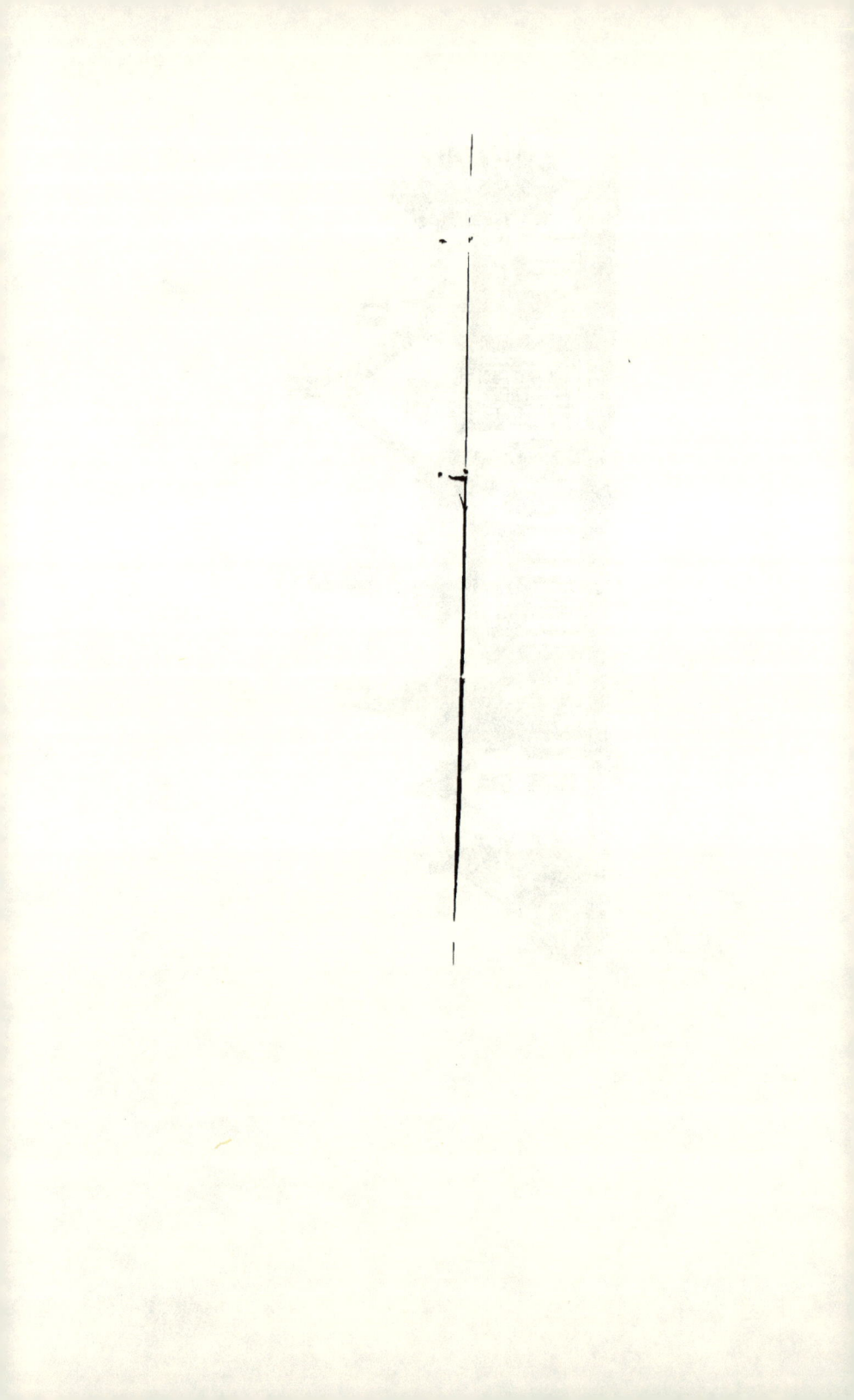

circumstances. But as this is a very important matter, and as the writer is most anxious not to over-state opportunities and advantages, it seems best to descend more fully into particulars. Taking, therefore, as an example (of which the facts are derived from personal knowledge) the Townships of Ascot and Orford and the County of Compton, which latter includes the Townships of Compton, Eaton, Bury, Lingwick, Clifton, and Westbury, with six others, farms with buildings and more or less cleared land can be purchased at prices from £100 to £1000, according to size and state of cultivation. Farms of 400 acres, with sawmills, good house, and out-buildings, within a mile or two of villages and easy access by excellent roads, are purchaseable at about £900. In some of the above-mentioned Townships a great many farms of say 100 acres, with 20 to 50 acres cleared, and buildings, can be had at from £100 to £200. These are the properties which would best suit most of our British small capitalists and yeomen, who could take out only a very moderate capital to start with, because these would not be able to settle upon the selected *wild lands* (purchasable at seven or eight shillings per acre) so cheaply as persons who are already experienced in the occupations of the country. At the same time, the present occupants, consisting generally of the persons who have made those clearings, are, for the most part, willing to re-commence on new lots, selling their already partially-cleared lands to successors more skilled than themselves in agriculture, though less fitted profitably to make fresh inroads into the forests. So far as the writer can judge from his own knowledge of facts and the reliable testimony of others, the above plan of procedure can be most safely recommended to British farmers of the class and amount of means referred to. Of such, it is known that thousands in Britain subsist in anxiety if not in absolute penury, to whom, having the comparatively small capital required for the first purchase of farm and stock, with a surplus adequate to their family wants until they get in their first harvest, a removal to the Eastern Townships would be attended with plenty and comfort. The cheapness of food and of all the actual necessaries of life, combined with access to the other advantages stated in the fore-going pages, would undoubtedly make the country to them a veritable land of promise.

In connection with what is said above about settling on lands wholly uncleared, it should be distinctly understood by the intending emigrant that the *Government Free Grants* are of that kind. They are offered only to actual settlers, who must reside upon their lots a certain time, and during that period bring a certain quantity under cultivation. This affords the opportunities to both parties referred to above, as it enables the man who sells his partially cleared land to the new comer to take up a fresh lot, without purchase. It is quite true, however, that persons only conversant with British modes of agriculture have gone into the backwoods of Canada and eventually succeeded in effecting comfortable settlements. But as a general rule the other method—that of settling on partially cleared land, is likely to prove the more economical to the small British capitalist.

For British farmers and yeomen of more considerable means, whose thoughts have been directed towards emigration, whether through failure of crops, increasing families, or deficiency of profit on their business, enough has been said to shew that these could at once step into a sphere of existence where most of their anxieties would cease ; where one-half of their present capital would suffice for establishing themselves on good farms to supply a comfortable living, and the other half, invested, would yield revenue for educating their sons and starting them in life with prospects not open to them in Britain. It is unnecessary here to dwell upon the larger opportunities of usefulness in all local, municipal, and political affairs that would at once present themselves in their adopted country. But on the subject of investments it is perhaps well to say, that *eight* per cent on perfectly good security is readily procurable by those who lay out money at interest in the Eastern Townships.

In the rural parts of England, as is well known, a ratio of capital of from £5 to £10 per acre is required in order to *rent* a farm ; so that if we take the case of a person farming about 500 acres, we might assign £4500 as the capital needed. Of this amount less than *one-third* would enable the possessor to become *owner* of a very fine farm and good habitation in the Townships, with a money income besides to assure and perpetuate the respectability, comforts, and the highest social advantages attending the enjoyment of a moderate competency.

In consequence of the establishment of the local University, and of the School founded in connection with it, as well as the free opportunities now accessible throughout the Townships, an English gentleman can now establish himself in the country on a footing of comfort to himself and family, and giving his sons an education of the highest order, on a capital which in the old country would scarcely yield revenue enough to pay one boy's expenses at Eton or Rugby.

At the same time, the writer would not desire it to be assumed that persons of any class, removing from Britain to a Colonial home in the Townships, would not in some degree experience sensations of *longing*, and even occasional regret, when their minds reverted to circumstances by which they were previously surrounded. The hallowed associations which bring up the scenes of one's youth and intercourse with former friends in the dear land of one's birth, cannot be flung aside like an old garment the moment it ceases to suit present requirements. They must recur in an experience of young colonial life, when this is placed in comparison with the time-honoured usages of England. But it is a fact that living under British Law, surrounded by British Institutions, and in the midst of a people who aspire at handing down the British name unstained to the latest posterity, is calculated to mitigate and to do away with any acerbity that might, under other conditions, prove intolerable. The knowledge, too, that Britain is within ten days' sail, instead of four or five weeks when the earlier settlers came to Canada, removes that sense of exile by which, as we read, they were often impressed. On the contrary, few persons from the old country who have lived in the Townships some years, in the enjoyment of health and moderate prosperity, would be found willing to resume a residence in Britain, where, to speak generally, there is more anxiety and even suffering on account of the mere necessaries of life in a single small city than would be met with in Canada from one end of the Province to the other. Without questioning the presence of what is good and great and venerable in English society, it is plain to every thoughtful observer, that a large emigration alone can sensibly afford relief from evils pressing upon it in all quarters. As some *must* emigrate, and as others *desire* to do so, impelled by various causes short of absolute necessity, there does not appear to be any good reason for laying much stress upon minor drawbacks growing out of the feelings alluded to, and which, after all, are for the most part temporary, and as nothing, compared with those occasioned by the suffering inevitable in an overcrowded population.

From the statements made in the foregoing pages persons of intelligence intending to remove from Britain to her nearest colonies can judge for themselves how far the Eastern Townships of Lower Canada offer the facilities they need. It will be seen from the incidental remarks made and the character of the information furnished that the writer has by no means solely in view the classes of emigrants chiefly referred to in the publications issued by Companies and by the Government authorities. In addition to capitalists with large means for embarking in manufactures and mining, *private gentlemen* of moderate fortune, as well as the better class of British farmers, under any inducement whatever for emigrating, will infer that the country is quite in a state of preparedness to meet their views also. Leaving Britain these need not dread that they are putting behind them for ever the refinements and other concomitants of civilized life. On the contrary, the writer feels able to assure such that in all probability they would for the most part enjoy the change on various accounts, but chiefly because of the extended sphere of usefulness in which they would be placed amongst a people thoroughly in earnest in their appreciation of the blessings of civil and religious liberty, and who under their free government and with their valuable municipal privileges have already achieved a good start in the occupation of the avenues leading to a well-grounded state of social happiness.

The exercise of the Legal and several other professions is so regulated by the laws of the Province that gentlemen dependent on these callings for a livelihood could scarcely expect to benefit themselves by coming to the Townships. In fact, the excellent Provincial Schools for the education of professional men form a source of supply adequate to the demands of the country. It is, however, barely possible that competent medical practitioners to whom, coming from any part of the British dominions, the Boards of the Province are authorized to grant a licence to enter upon practice immediately, might here and there find an opening. But such opportunities may be stated to be rare.

As respects the prospects existing at present in the Eastern Townships for emigrants of the class dependent upon labour and having no capital, it is difficult with any degree of confidence to say what they are. If the anticipations should be realized relating to a more considerable influx of those other classes which have been previously mentioned, then it is obvious there would arise a very great demand. The official returns issued a short time back by the Canadian Bureau of Agriculture furnish a statement of the numbers immediately required in 24 municipalities of *Eastern Canada*. They include farm labourers, female servants, boys and girls over 13 years of age, in all, it is stated, 1660 persons—but how many of these would be directed to the Townships does not appear. It should be distinctly understood that while there is customarily a demand for the services of respectable domestic servants there is little or no encouragement to induce females of higher pretensions to go out in the expectation of immediate employment on arrival. Educated ladies, such as governesses, when they do obtain engagements, usually do so through the agency of private recommendation.

The writer cannot close these remarks without alluding to a topic which has of late been the subject of much discussion—*Canadian Loyalty*. To speak of this matter here, in reference to Canada, generally, is unnecessary, as the disparaging insinuations which had been permitted to intrude in some quarters in England have been satisfactorily refuted in the published letters and speeches of Canadians now on a visit to this country.

But as respects the people of the Townships, it may be said they are not surpassed by any in the Province in the amount of their attachment to their Queen, constitution, and country. They have manifested this on many occasions. The Queen's birthday is customarily observed with demonstrations, bonfires, &c., in the towns and villages. When subscriptions have been made in the colonies in behalf of national objects and sympathies, the Township people have shared in such efforts in proportion to their ability. Several corps of volunteers and riflemen were raised among them to contribute to the defence of the country, when, recently, there were apprehensions of a war with the United States. In fact, they are no more deficient of loyalty than are the inhabitants of any English county.

It should be stated, however, that while there can be no doubt but that the people of the Eastern Townships would, in any just cause, not fall behind any other community in the Province, or fail in doing all they could in their own defence and to aid their country, still, the peaceable nature of their avocations, the peculiar position of their territory, as well as the long-continued friendly intercourse which has subsisted between themselves and the contiguous States, all unite in rendering the prospect of a war between England and that country extremely repugnant to the feelings of the majority. It is plainly quite natural that such should be the case, and that no imputation of disloyalty can be justly founded upon it. To allege the contrary would be as unreasonable as to impute disloyalty to the vast majority of the inhabitants of the British Isles for entertaining feelings which would make them deplore the breaking out of a war with their near neighbours, the people of France.

The writer has pleasure in appending the substance of some letters, from a resident of the Eastern Townships, of a few years standing, to a correspondent in England. Although confined almost entirely to a single locality, the statements are generally applicable, and may serve to assist the reader in forming an opinion about social and other characteristics.

APPENDIX.

Lennoxville, Eastern Townships,
Sept. 3rd, 1861.

MY DEAR P.

So I find my guess was an over true one. I had touched the sore in hinting that the arrival of No. 10 and 11 was not quite so joyous an event as the welcome of previous additions to the old stock. It has had one good effect, however, in inducing you to think whether, after all, it would not be better to move the whole of the incumbrances to a cheaper country. Rely on it, such is the result: their arrival will prove to you the greatest blessing that has ever been sent to you. Gladly will I answer your queries; and though I confess to a strong bias to my new country, I will give you as honest an opinion as I can. I will confine myself as much as possible to facts; and as you will of course make enquiries from other sources, before finally deciding on moving, you will easily ascertain if my facts are indeed facts.

You say you are surprised at my former descriptions of the English appearance of the country—of the English tone of feeling, society, manners, &c.—so different from what you had supposed. You must please remember that Canada is a large country. To give an honest and fair description, each writer must confine himself to an account of that part with which he is personally acquainted. His description may therefore differ as much from another account, equally honestly given, only from another place, as would be the case with two accounts of life in Cornwall and the North of Scotland. Persons reading descriptions of this part of the country, and going west, have no right to consider themselves misled, if they find the reality differ from their expectations, and vice versâ. Now I have no intention of writing to you about *all* Canada. I have lived in the West, have seen other parts of Canada, and have formed my own opinion as to where I myself prefer to reside., Others, however, may have different tastes.

Lennoxville is an exceedingly pretty little country village, consisting of one large wide street, with another crossing it at right angles. The centre of the village is a large open square, with two large clean comfortable hotels. On the left of the road, a little out of the village, stands the brick church, with its high tin-crowned steeple. Opposite are the pretty English looking cottages of some of our gentry. Going through the village by the cross-road, we come to the Railway crossing (the Montreal and Portland part of the Grand Trunk system), which runs through the village: then comes the house of our good clergyman, and next that of one of our University Professors. Then we pass through one of the bridges over the river Massawhippi, peculiar in build to this part of the country, being entirely covered and closed in at the sides. Beyond this, on a rising ground, about 100 yards from the bridge, stands the imposing (for Canada) pile of the College buildings—built of red brick, in the Gothic style, with its pretty chapel flanking it at one extremity, and looking down on a wide reach of the river St. Francis, and the junction of that river and the Massawhippi; and beyond this may be seen the churches and chapels of our county town of Sherbrooke, about three miles distant. The village lies in a hollow, with well cultivated hill sides rising from the valley, very prettily wooded, with the farm houses dotted about on each clearing.

The village boasts its three or four excellent shops or stores, as called here, where almost every thing can be obtained; a post office, two forges, saddler, watch-maker (who is also a first-rate photographic artist), and a very neat railway-station and large freight house. It has also a considerable saw-mill worked both by water and steam power. In the cross street is a neat Wesleyan Chapel; and the plain but most useful Town Hall, the public room of which is in continual request for meetings, singing classes, &c. stands in the main street. The Inns are large, clean and comfortable. I never knew greater comfort or attention in any English country inn than I have experienced at the Albion, and its charges are so moderate as to astonish any one who has lately come from England. Three shillings a day (currency not above half-a-crown sterling) provides excellent bed and sitting-room—meals three times a day with meat at each, and everything properly cooked. We have a Doctor in the village, but strange to say, and almost incredible, neither a lawyer nor a rat! We boast of being head-quarters of three companies of Volunteer Rifles, all uniformed at their own expense, but supplied with arms by the Government. The uniform is the regulation uniform, almost exactly similar to the 60th. Connected with these is the excellent Brass Band belonging to the First Company, and consisting of 19 performers. The village also has a large covered *Rink*—that is, a covered Skating Room—80 feet by 40, with dressing-rooms attached, heated by a stove. In winter this is the great meeting-place for all the young folks (and many old too) of the neighbourhood—and a pretty gay sight it is to see the beauty of Lennoxville enjoying this most fascinating and healthy amusement. Very few places in Canada, except the large cities, possess Rinks like those of Lennoxville and Sherbrooke.

About three miles north of Lennoxville, lower down the St. Francis, is our county town of Sherbrooke, a large thriving bustling town, through which the river Magog pours, tumbling from one fall to another—affording perhaps the finest and most valuable water power to be found in all

Canada. It principally belongs to the British American Land Company—who own a large breadth of valuable land in this part of the Townships, and whose affairs are placed under the spirited and enlightened management of their present Chief Commissioner, R. W. Henneker, Esq., who is ever anxious to advance the true interests of the Townships. A few miles further on the Railway are the Brompton Mills.

To the south and south-east of Lennoxville is the thriving manufacturing village of Waterville, distant about six miles, and beyond this, other centres of important agricultural neighbourhoods, where farming is carried on on really scientific principles, and which contains farms second to few either as regards stock or high cultivation in any part of the world. I will answer your questions about the College and School here in my next letter, and also about prices, climate, &c.

Lennoxville, Eastern Townships,
November 3rd, 1861.

My DEAR P.

I now proceed to perform the promise contained in my last letter, and shall make up for my past delay by writing to you this time a long one.

To begin with a point which naturally interests you very much, viz. how you are to get good education for your boys, I will say a little about the College here and the Grammar School founded by and closely connected with it.

It has been established nearly 20 years, and is probably destined to be to this Province what Oxford and Cambridge have been and are to England. It has a Royal Charter with the privilege of granting all degrees. It is conducted under regulations prescribed by its Corporation. The Principal of the University is Dr. Nicolls, of Oriel College, Oxford—whose residence forms the left wing of the buildings. He is also Classical Professor. The Vice-Principal is Professor H. Miles, Professor of Mathematics, and Natural Philosophy. The Divinity chair, which has been vacant, for a short time, is about to be filled by a gentleman from England, not yet, or only just appointed. The Rev. W. Williams is Professor of Belles Lettres, with charge of the Junior Department and Grammar School. The examination for degrees takes place yearly, and they are conferred at the Meeting of Convocation in June. The Students have their private rooms, attending lectures from the various Professors. There is a large and very handsome Dining Hall, where the Students have their meals under the superintendence of some Professor. There is daily service in the Chapel, a gem of its kind. The subjects of study are quite as advanced as at the English Universities. The course extends over three years. A gold medal prize has been instituted through the generous endowment of the Prince of Wales.

Many of the Students are residing in College. The charges are very moderate.

The College fees for tuition are $27 or £5. 10s, and for their rooms, use of the College Library and firing, $9 or £1. 16s per annum. Students who have parents or friends residing in the neighbourhood (and this is a very important consideration for families settling here) may attend the Lectures, only paying the tuition fee of $19, having all the advantages as if resident.

Though Bishop's College is of course founded in connection with the Church of England, no intolerance of religious feeling is shewn. None are required to attend the Chapel services who have a conscientious objection, and the degrees are not limited to the members of our Church.

Closely connected with the College, and situate in the Quadrangle, but distinct from it as a building, is the High School of Bishop's College, numbering at present above 100 boys, under the charge of the Rector, the Rev. J. W. Williams. Under his management, the School has already taken a high position, and is drawing scholars from other British Colonies, as well as from Western Canada. In the course of study, *French*, being a necessary qualification for success in every profession or business in this Province, is specially provided for. Besides the Rector, the School has two English and one French Master.

The charge for boys boarding on the establishment is only $3 or 12s sterling per week, and the tuition fees are $36 a year, or £7. 5s. Washing 1s a week. The whole expense for 40 weeks amounts to £35. 5s. Several families in the vicinity accommodate boys whose parents prefer this, at a charge of from $3 to $5 per week. The great advantage, however, to families residing in the neighbourhood, is that they can board their sons at home, and have only to pay $36, or £7. 5s, for the tuition fees, for which they will receive as high a class education as any school in the world can offer—the school having the great advantage of the supervision and assistance of College Professors of the highest standing in addition to the teaching of the masters.

The boys have a Drill Instructor, and they have proved their loyalty by establishing a Corps of Volunteer Rifles, which has been enthusiastically supported. Three of the elder boys were gazetted as *Captain*, *Lieutenant*, and *Ensign*.

All English manly games are in full use here. The boys have their cricket clubs, football matches, &c., besides skating, snow-shoeing, &c., all manly, athletic games being encouraged.

The advantages for education cannot be surpassed in any country neighbourhood, either here or in England, whilst the cheap cost at which it can be obtained, especially for residents in or near Lennoxville, renders it a most desirable locality for families such as yours.

Lennoxville is a particularly healthy neighbourhood. Fever and ague, that bane of the west, is utterly unknown here; and notwithstanding our cold winters, coughs and colds are very uncommon. Our houses are well-warmed, either by open fire places or stoves, and so little is the out of door cold thought of, that English ladies drive about in open sleighs with little change from English winter costume, except perhaps in using a fur cap instead of a bonnet. With the thermometer between 20 and 30 degrees below zero we have large parties turning out to enjoy our lovely moonlight nights, and none suffer by it.

We are fortunate in having a very excellent society in and around Lennoxville. The Professors of the College, all of them English University men, and their families, would alone form the nucleus of a superior circle of society, but in addition there are many English families settled here and in Sherbrooke who contribute greatly to render it agreeable.

Lennoxville is a particularly cheap neighbourhood for all the necessaries of life, the prices of which contrast most favourably with those in the old country, and the quality is equally good. Beef from October to March costs 4½ to 5 cents, or 2d to 2½d sterling—from April to September it is higher, about 6 cents, or 3d per lb.; mutton, 6 to 8 cents (3d to 4d); lamb, 6 to 10 cents (3d to 5d); pork, 5 to 7 cents (2½d to 3½d); potatoes, 10d to 1s 6d per bushel; butter, 7d to 9d per lb.; flour and other articles in proportion. We get excellent fresh fish from Portland at 3 cents, or 1½d per lb., consisting of cod, haddock, mackerel, &c. Lobsters and oysters are also very cheap. Raspberries and strawberries grow wild in the greatest abundance and of delicious flavour. They are brought to the doors in great quantities by the children for sale. All English garden vegetables succeed well, especially asparagus.

There is a very general complaint about the difficulty of getting good servants, but still such are to be found. Wages for a cook are $4 to $7 per month; housemaids, $3 to $5; nurses, $3 to $6; waitress, $5 to $7. Men servants in livery are unknown in the country parts of Canada.

As every English gentleman comes to Canada with the British mania for being a landowner, I will now mention the price of farms that have lately been sold in this neighbourhood. I must premise, however, that I think that it would be better for the great majority of emigrants, especially those who look principally to educational advantages, to content themselves with a few acres of land (there are hundreds of beautiful sites) near the village, on which to build cottages to suit their own tastes. A very good house in the Gothic style, with high roofs lined outside with brick (a very warm and cheap style of building) would cost from $800 to $1200, £200 to £350 sterling. If without the brick casing it would be considerably cheaper. In fact, a good two-storied cottage with four rooms on the ground floor and five bed-rooms above, with kitchen in a side wing, built on stone foundations, and well cellared and surrounded by a verandah, has been built for $800, or £160 sterling. The land would cost according to situation near the village from $20 to $400 per acre, £4. to £80.

During the last two years the following farms have been sold:—

A farm of 450 acres, 8 miles from Lennoxville, 150 acres cleared, with good house, outbuildings, barns, &c.; very good land, for $3400, or £680 sterling.

A farm of 115 acres, 4 miles distant, 40 acres cleared, with good log hut, cellared, and good barn, for $4000, or £800 sterling, payable by instalments in 4 years.

A farm of 360 acres, close to the village, 200 acres cleared, an excellent stock farm, indifferent house and buildings, $6000, £1200. This farm has some beautiful sites for villas.

A farm of 600 acres, 5 miles from Lennoxville, 300 acres cleared, and 150 acres of rich interval land, excellent house and outbuildings, $10,000, or £2000 sterling.

A farm of 115 acres, close to the village, 80 cleared, with a large Gothic brick house, stables, barns, farm cottage, $6000, or £1200 sterling. The house is most substantially built, with 8 foot cellars under the whole; and one seldom to be found in any of the country parts of Canada.

A farm of 400 acres, about 10 miles from Lennoxville, near the pretty village of Cashahire, 80 acres cleared, with comfortable cottage, farmbuildings, &c., $1400, or £280.

A farm of 110 acres, situated on the flat land near the river, about one mile from Lennoxville, with excellent house, farm-buildings of every kind, very rich land, $5000, or £1000 sterling.

There are several other farms within half to 3 miles from Lennoxville, which might be bought at from $800 to $2000, £160 to £400, according to the value of the buildings upon them.

There is but a very trifling expense incurred in legal charges for land purchases in Canada, a simple form, half printed, gives the buyer all the title he requires. This is entered in the Municipal Registry, in which all mortgages must also be recorded, to make the security complete.

The cost of stocking a farm, with 80 to 100 acres cleared, would amount to about $500 to $800—£130 to £160 sterling.

88

Firewood costs $1 per cord measuring 8 feet by 4 and 4. The consumption of a moderate sized house would range from 30 to 80 cords. Almost every farm has its sugary, comprising from 300 to 1000 maple trees, which average from ½ to 2 lb. per tree, according to the season. This sugar is worth about 8 cents, or 4½d. per lb. There is a very good brewery in Lennoxville. Groceries are cheaper than in England.

I have now, I think, answered all your questions, my dear P., and hoping you will soon make up your mind to join us, remain ever yours, &c.

Lennoxville, Feb. 14, 1862.

MY DEAR P.

So the great decision has been really and truly taken, and both you and Mrs. P. have made up your minds to follow my advice, and exchange scarcity for plenty, a deficient for an abundant income. I can well enter into your account of the many *pros* and *cons* to be weighed before you decided, and can feel for the painful opposition of well-meaning friends which you have had already to encounter, and which it will take years of success here to overcome. It is certainly by far the most painful phase of emigration to part with dearly loved friends.

One word about what you should bring out with you. Do not bring furniture of any kind, except it be some old favourite bureau. Pianos, even, can be better and cheaper got here. Bring everything you have in the shape of clothing; Canada is a glorious place for using up old clothing. Bring a good supply of boots and shoes for all the family. Get yourself a pair of knee boots, large enough for two pairs of worsted stockings. Bring lots of blankets, house linen, crockery, glassware, flannel, calico. Bring good English saddles, and any fairish harness you may have but do not bring any new. Of course a good gun and a rifle would be useful. If a fly fisherman, bring rods, lines, &c., but no trout flies; here they use them three times the size of our English flies. Bring carpets, rugs, &c. Books are cheap here, being American editions of standard English works.

I have now said my say. I have told you facts so far as facts are useful. Where it becomes a matter of opinion or fancy, I have given my honest candid opinion.

May we meet soon, my dear P., in the New World.

Yours ever, &c.

THE END.

G. NORMAN, PRINTER, MAIDEN LANE, COVENT GARDEN, LONDON.

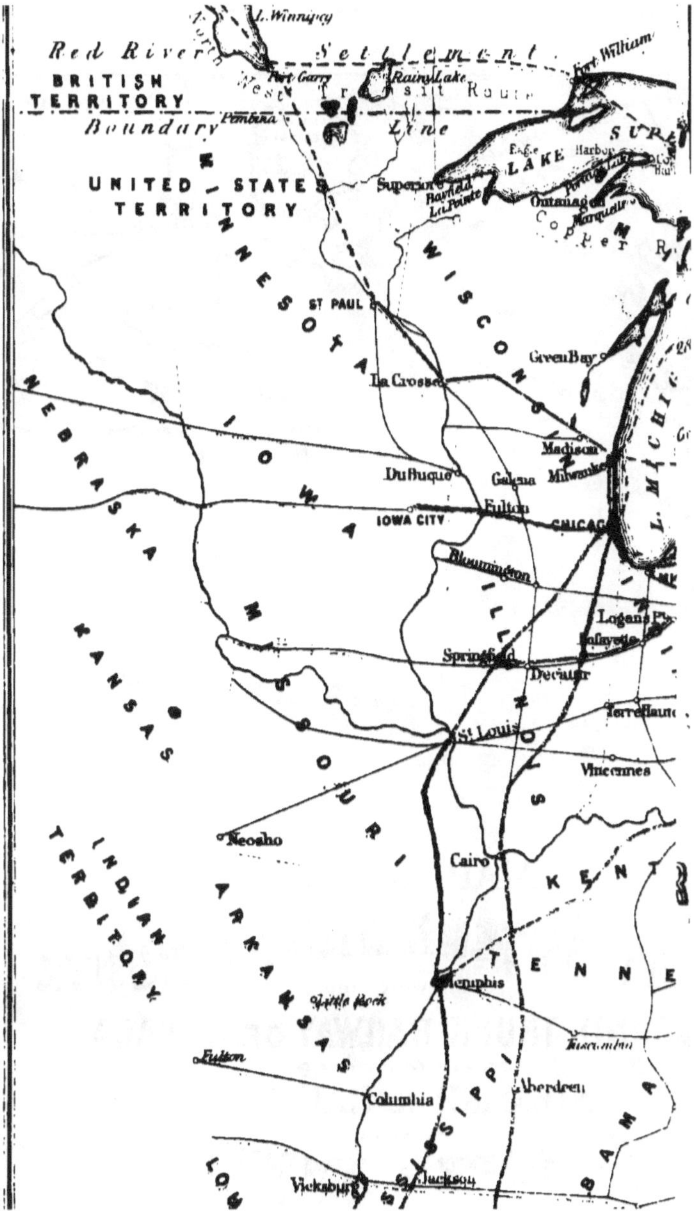
L. Winnipeg
Red River Settlement
BRITISH TERRITORY
Fort Garry
Rainy Lake
Fort William
North West Transit Route
Pembina
Boundary Line
LAKE SUPERIOR
Superior
Bayfield
La Pointe
Eagle Harbor
Portage Lake
Ontanagon
Marquette
Copper R.
UNITED STATES TERRITORY
MINNESOTA
ST PAUL
WISCONSIN
Green Bay
La Crosse
NEBRASKA
IOWA
Madison
Milwaukee
DuBuque
Galena
Fulton
IOWA CITY
CHICAGO
L. MICHIGAN
Bloomington
ILLINOIS
Logans Port
Lafayette
Springfield
Decatur
Terre Haute
KANSAS
MISSOURI
St Louis
Vincennes
INDIAN TERRITORY
Neosho
Cairo
KENTUCKY
TENNESSEE
ARKANSAS
Memphis
Little Rock
Tuscumbia
Fulton
Aberdeen
Columbia
MISSISSIPPI
ALABAMA
Vicksburg
Jackson

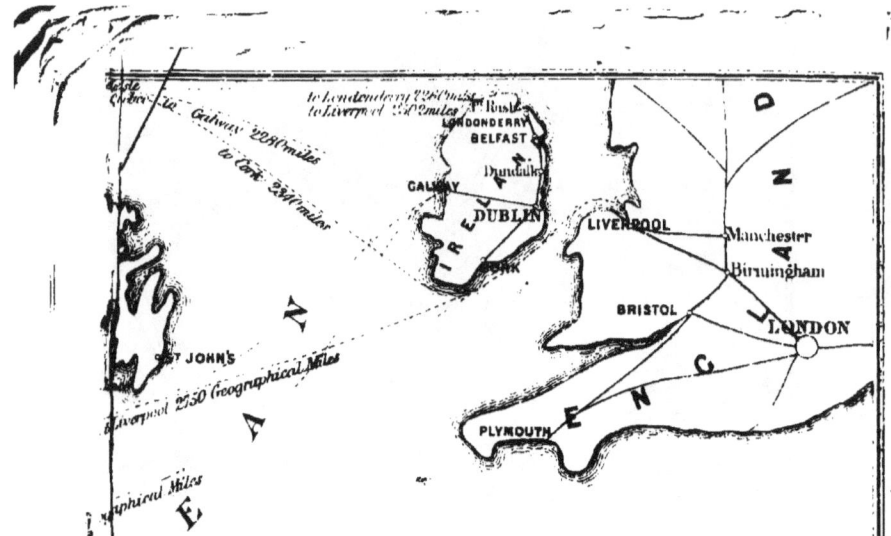

MAP OF THE

GREAT INTERNATIONAL ROUTE

Shewing the

GRAND TRUNK RAILWAY of CANADA,

and its Connections by

STEAMER & RAILWAY,

with

EUROPE & AMERICA

ADAMS & GEE. LITHO 23 MIDDLE S⸂ E.C.